Praise for *Lost on Mars*
Book one of

'… wondrous, strange and satis[…]

Mr Ripley's Enchanted Book
Reads 2015
'It's FANTASTIC, it's BRILLIANT, it's certainly strange and the plot will hit you in both the gut and the heart at the same time. It's thought provoking and very surreal … the more that I read, the more that I fell in love with this book… This is easily my favourite read of the year. It is a cracking space odyssey for the Young Adult audience and beyond. A unique outlook all wrapped in a disturbing fight for survival against a bleak and desolate landscape.'

One of *The Telegraph*'s Best YA Books of 2015
'The story is bold and you have to love a chapter that opens with the words: "It was late in our Martian autumn when we were allowed to hold the funeral for Grandma's leg." Lora, stubborn and complex, is at the heart of this first part of a trilogy about third-generation settlers on the desolate red planet. There's also a likeable and talkative robot called Toaster. It's also a novel about alienation. But watch out for the Martian flesh-eaters.'

The Independent's Best Summer Reads
'A wonderfully written sci-fi adventure about a pioneer family on the desert plains of the red planet, a terrifying, inhospitable world of massive dust storms. Then the disappearances begin. Grandma is taken and all that is left is her cybernetic leg. Completely irresistible.'
Patricia Duncker

'Paul Magrs's *Lost On Mars* is about Martian settlers being Disappeared by Martians. Funny, scary, and like Ray Bradbury crossed with Laura Ingalls Wilde[…] it will appeal to boys and Dr Who fans.'
Amanda Cra[…]

Paul Magrs grew up in Newton Aycliffe, County Durham and went to the University of Lancaster. He was a Senior Lecturer in English Literature and Creative Writing at UEA, running their famous MA course, and then at MMU in Manchester. Now he writes full time, at home in Levenshulme, where he lives with his partner Jeremy Hoad. He's written many children's and YA titles, including five *Doctor Who* novels with BBC Books, *Strange Boy*, *Exchange* and *Diary of a Doctor Who Addict*.

THE MARTIAN GIRL

First published in 2016
by Firefly Press
25 Gabalfa Road, Llandaff North, Cardiff, CF14 2JJ
www.fireflypress.co.uk

Text © Paul Magrs 2016

A CIP catalogue record of this book is available from the British Library.

Print ISBN 978-1-910080443
epub ISBN 978-1-910080450

*This book has been published with the support of the
Welsh Books Council.*

Typeset by: Elaine Sharples

Printed and bound by: Pulsio SARL

THE MARTIAN GIRL

PAUL MAGRS

Firefly

Prologue

My name is Lora and when I was a kid I lived in a house with my whole family on one of the red prairies of Mars. There was Ma and Da and my brother Al, my little sister Hannah and me. Plus there was Grandma, who was crazy, and Toaster, our sunbed, who helped out with everything from gathering the corn crop to battening down the electronic sealants when the great dust storms came.

When I was fifteen there was trouble in Our Town, which was the closest town to where we lived. People were getting Disappeared and there was a panic on.

I knew who was causing all the Disappearances. I knew because I saw them, dancing down the dusty streets at night. Tall, skinny creatures with glowing eyes, giggling in the Earth light. They were the Martian Ghosts and they were taking our people away, one by one.

They took away my grandma and then they took Da.

Those were terrible days. And I knew that we had to get away. If we stayed near Our Town and buried our heads in the red sand like the rest of them, we were doomed.

I was the only one who would take charge.

Me, Al, Ma and Hannah packed everything we could

fit into our hovercart, and we convinced a handful of brave souls to come with us. Together we faced the emptiness of the Martian wilderness and set off to find a new home.

To me, though, Mars wasn't just wild, it was beautiful. I knew that because of a secret. I knew it because of my secret friend, Sook, who had wings and strange eyes, just like a Martian Ghost. She was gentle and kind and she appeared at times like an angel or a giant moth, with these wonderful wings of hers. She would lift me up in her strong, skinny arms and fly me over the desert at night. This happened several times during the year I was fifteen and I saw more of Mars than maybe anyone in my family ever had. I saw its vastness and its beauty. It was a mysterious, deadly world.

But our little group became separated from each other. We were captured by lizard birds and taken deep underground to their caverns, and our brave party was torn apart.

My brother Al and I, together with Toaster, escaped to a new place. Sook carried us there. Mysteriously as ever, she took hold of us and flew us who knew how far, to a city we didn't even know existed. This was the City Inside, where the buildings were taller than we could imagine, everything was made of green glass, and it snowed red snow on the City streets almost every single day.

For five whole days we were heroes. We were the girl and boy who'd come wandering out of the desert, together with their kronky old robot. We were given a fine place to live and we could do whatever we wanted. It looked like our adventures were over.

Except ... I never felt quite at home in that City Inside. It wasn't just that I missed our prairie. I felt that things were being done and said and sorted out behind our backs.

It all felt kind of sinister to me.

Luckily, I made friends with a busker called Peter and his cat-dog Karl. They lived hidden away in a Den underneath a City park. Listening to Peter talk, I learned that the City Inside wasn't as shiny and lovely as it seemed.

Just as I had suspected.

Al got himself in favour with the fancy Graveley family, and got a job on the newspaper they owned. He started to change, to settle down. Toaster had himself repaired and fixed up. He was taken away by the Authorities and I was starting to think I'd never see him again.

I was invited to the University by a professor who wanted all my memories of growing up on the prairie for his archives. I went to his laboratory and he hooked me up to a machine. But I changed my mind. Why should I let them suck out all my memories? change to: With Peter's help, I jumped out of the machine and ran away.

And then, at Christmas, the strangest thing of all happened. A trail of clues ... a little bit of finding out ... and I was drawn to a building of dark, shrouded windows, hidden behind the department stores of the commercial district. At the top of metal stairways in this warren of small dwellings, right at the very top, there was a certain door.

And behind that door I found two very unexpected faces. Da and Grandma! They had been living in the City Inside for months. This was where they had been Disappeared to. And they were delighted to see me and Al. But where was Ma? Where was Hannah? We didn't know, and we couldn't tell them. Our family wasn't whole yet and we couldn't be completely happy until it was.

But for now it was Christmas and we celebrated. We made the best of things and tried to make it feel like home, although the City Inside was never our home.

If I ever got the chance, I decided I'd get away from this City.

If I ever get the opportunity, I'll find my way back home.

1

My whole family is on the run.

We're not all great at running. Hannah's my baby sister and we have to take turns to pick her up. Those of us who are faster stay behind to help each other. That's the way it is.

We can hear the cracks and booms of gunfire behind us. The raucous yells of the hunters and their shouts of triumph.

It's hard to run on this ground. Steaming swampland. Viscous, oozing purple mud. The vegetation is thick and red and every now and then we can hide and catch our breath.

The bullets shriek and sizzle through the humid air. They're still after us. They won't give up. It's all a game to them. We're gonna wind up dead.

Ma is hysterical. Her limbs fail and she wants to give up. She's sobbing as my brother Al stands there with the baby. Da is trying to shake sense into her. If they catch us we're dead. Simple as that. Everything will have been for nothing. We have to keep on. We have to survive.

Surprisingly, Grandma is on her feet and ready to run again. The danger has given her extra life and her eyes are shining. 'Come on, come on. We've got to run. We can't stop now.'

Bringing up the rear is Toaster. He's our loyal servant and our protector. The kronky robot sunbed, who's just about the oldest member of our family. He would lay down his life for us. He's striding across the perilous marsh with his circuits fizzing and his ancient joints sparking. He's leading us through the vast swamp, sure that he can get us safely through to the other side and out of the range of the crazy hunters who are after us.

'I'm sorry, this is all my fault,' says Toaster as he lumbers through the long grasses. 'Those are Antique Hunters after us. They're after me! It's me they want!'

My da shakes his head grimly. 'They won't stop till we're all dead.'

Ma cries out at this, part horror, part outrage. She hauls herself to her feet and holds out her arms for Hannah. 'I'm all right. I can go on. We can't let them take us. We've come this far…'

A steely determination comes over her. We plough on, with the gunfire and the distant, mocking laughter ringing in our ears.

We are tough, me and my family. We've already had to survive so much. And we can surely survive this…

'Lora! Lora…!'

Al was yelling at me. For some reason he had stopped running and was peering down into my face and shaking my shoulders.

'Lora! You were shouting out again. You were having your dreams again…'

I pushed him away. Feeling groggy, I sat up on my makeshift bed and groaned.

I was in the living room of the flat where Da and Grandma lived. I looked around and the dark tree was still there, and the loops of straggly tinsel and homemade paper chains. I was safe.

'You were really yelling out this time,' Al laughed. 'That's the third night in a row.'

I got up woozily. Then I headed to the galley kitchen for a glass of water. Every surface was littered with used crockery and cooking pans and dishes. Grandma was a bit slapdash with cleaning stuff up.

Three nights of dreams. Every night the same dream. Our whole family being pursued through a hideous, lurid swamp. The Antique Hunters with their ancient guns firing lead bullets at us and never letting up. Three nights I'd slept on Grandma's settee and woken in this cold sweat.

My brother Al thought it was hilarious.

Da showed up, looking concerned. 'What's going on? It's not even light outside. What was all the noise?'

For a second it was like we were two little kids again. Da coming in, tying up his dressing gown, ready to give us both a telling off for disturbing the household. I even smiled at the memory. But Al and me, we weren't little kids any more. I was sixteen that year and he was fourteen. And we no longer lived in our Homestead on the prairie. We lived in the City now and everything had changed.

'I … I'm sorry, Da. It was me. Bad dreams.'

He came over to hug me. I waved him away. I didn't want fussing over. 'It's no surprise you get nightmares,' he sighed. 'The things you two have gone through. The things you must have seen.'

'It wasn't so bad,' I said.

But it was. Our journey from Our Town through the Martian wilderness with Ma and Hannah had been terrifyingly dangerous. Why was I trying to play it down?

In the living room Al was bundling up his bedroll and stashing away the sheets and pillows. 'Christmas is over now,' he said as we drank the strong, milky coffee Da had made for us. 'I guess it's time we got back to normal. I've got to get back to my job today.'

I knew that he meant he had to make peace between himself and the Graveley family. There had been a falling out, and he wanted to get back in their favour.

Da wanted to hear more about Al's job at *The City Insider*, which was a big, important newspaper. But Al didn't look keen to talk as he gobbled up his breakfast.

'My little boy – working already! And at an important desk job!' Da sounded mightily impressed. 'And there's his da, just an old farmer. I'm proud of you, son.'

Al ducked his head and looked abashed. I watched him and realised that he hadn't yet told Da and Grandma anything about his new life in the City Inside. He had kept quiet about his friendship with the Graveley family who ran the newspaper. What was more, he hadn't said a single word about being a sort of boyfriend to Tillian, the Graveleys' daughter. Da would have thought the same as I did. Al was much too young to have a proper girlfriend. Even if people did grow up quicker here in the City, and even if life was paced much faster than we were used to. He was still just a kid, really.

Al knew they'd disapprove as well, and I reckoned that was why he hadn't said much about what he'd been up to in the months our family had all been apart.

I guess we'd all changed some. I know I had, though it was hard to gauge it. I didn't feel so different inside but, during the few days of the Christmas break, I'd caught both Da and Grandma watching me, studying me. It was as if they were trying to size up this more independent person I'd become since they Disappeared.

That's what happened to them, you see. We believed that the Martian Ghosts had risen up from the depths of the dustbowl to claim them. I'd even seen those long, stringy, eerie ghosts in the moonlight myself, dancing

9

down Main Street in the silence of the night, looking for souls to snatch away.

But though we were right to set out to start a new life, there were certain things we were wrong about. Important things. For example, our belief that Da and Grandma were dead. They were not. They were just living in this City where the Martians had brought them. Deep in the heart of Bolingbroke District, where the buildings were high and the stores were gaudy. They were here the whole time, just waiting for me to find them.

I supposed Al was right. It was time to return to our flat across the City. We couldn't make Christmas last forever. But it had been wonderful, staying there for a few days with Da and Grandma, in this tiny flat at the top of the fire escape. The cinnamon-coloured snow had been drifting down, day after day, and at one point we even thought we might be snowed in.

It was like the old days in so many ways. It was like the Christmases of the past, in our little house miles from civilisation, when it was just our family and no one else. For a few days we'd been able to push away the thought that there were millions of souls all around us. The City Inside was teeming with a multitude of human beings and other creatures. With Martians, too.

Of course, Ma was missing. And Hannah. And Ruby, Grandma's friend. It could never truly be like Christmas without them. Late in the evenings I thought about how Ma used to play her miniature harp to us. She'd play all the complicated songs handed down to us by our ancestors from Earth. This Christmas we'd had to make do with Grandma's cracked old voice instead. She sang Christmas songs and also songs about how it was her generation and her people who first came to Mars.

Those songs rang a bit hollow now. Now that I knew that her people weren't the first after all.

But Grandma tried to entertain us as best she could. 'Peter's enjoying my singing!' she laughed and cawed, rocking in her chair by the gas fire. She pointed to my new best friend and cackled like crazy. 'He appreciates a golden oldie when he sees one, don't you, son?'

She was even flirting with him. I'd met Peter in the marketplace underneath the building where Al and I were living nowadays. Peter had become a good friend, and someone I quickly came to rely upon for advice and help in this new and strange place. He and his pet dog Karl (or was he a cat? I could never be sure) were homeless, I thought, at first. But it turned out they lived somewhere called the Den, which was underground, underneath a park, somewhere on the east side of the City, in Eventide District. Now Peter had been drawn into the orbit of my family and the strange things that were happening to us. But I think he was pleased to spend Christmas with us. He said that it was much better than the gloomy time he would have had in the Den without Karl.

'He's lost his little friend, his little pet,' Grandma crooned sympathetically. 'I know what it's like. You must be very sad right now.'

The thing was, Grandma sounded sympathetic, but there was a devilish glint in her eye. I was reminded that I had never really quite trusted Grandma. I recalled very well how she had been apt to go crazy every once in a while. In those times she would say and do some very alarming things indeed.

By Boxing Day Peter had already returned to his Den. He was keen not to outstay his welcome. As polite as ever, he thanked Da and Grandma and kissed me goodbye at the top of the fire escape.

'I'll call on you,' I promised. 'When I get back. We can start looking for Karl again…'

He nodded and smiled, but it looked to me as if he had given up all hope of seeing his beloved pet again. Karl was missing and it was all my fault. The little cat-dog-thing had been shivering with pneumonia or something on the last day Peter had seen him, and he was helpless, with his tangled and malformed limbs. Even on the best days Peter had to carry him about. But it was selfish me who insisted that we leave him outside the university buildings on a cold and wet night, so that Peter could come and be my back-up when I entered the hallowed and scary halls of the Department of True Life Stories. When we had escaped from there, we'd found that Karl was gone. Only his blanket and his little lead were lying there in the crimson slush. It was all my fault. I wonder, if I had been Peter, whether I'd find it so easy to forgive me?

Already days had slipped by and I was preparing to return home later than I'd intended. The lure of burying myself in Christmas and family and sleeping on the settee under the tree for nights on end had proved too strong. But it was no good. Even though my head ached with those nightmares I could still see whenever I closed my eyelids, I must pull myself together and return to my ordinary life.

'I'll come back soon,' I told Grandma and Da. 'And then you two will have to come and visit me in Stockpot District. Come and see my flat on the 202nd floor!'

Da looked at me, amazed. 'Just imagine a daughter of mine living somewhere as swanky as that!' he said. 'I'm very proud of you, Lore.'

'How does she afford it, is what I want to know,' muttered Grandma.

We were standing in their narrow hallway and I was preparing to leave and brave the freezing wind and snow. The climate outside was a little less gentle and Christmas card-like today. Through the iced windows it looked savage and bleak. I told Grandma, 'The Authorities put us in our flat when we first arrived. Me and Al. They looked after us. Gave us somewhere to live. They made a big fuss of us walking out of the desert…'

Grandma looked puzzled at my words. 'I still don't get it. Why would they just give you a fancy place to live? Huh? What do they want from you? There's gotta be something. No one gets something for nothing. That's what I've learned.'

Da rolled his eyes and hugged me one last time. 'Never mind your grandma. She's just suspicious about everyone.'

As I left, I thought again about how Da had been completely unaware that Al and I had been celebrities for about five minutes when we first arrived. Why, we'd been on the news channels and in the magazines and newspapers for almost a whole week. For a little while it was like everyone was fascinated by the boy and girl from the wilderness. In fact, that was how Al had met Tillian; she was the reporter sent to talk to us, to get an exclusive on our story. When I'd told Da and Grandma this they just shook their heads slowly and told me that they never bothered with the news or the papers. They didn't really follow anything much going on in their new City. They were used to simpler things and they had their lives to get on with. The things that happened in the City Inside didn't really touch them.

When Da said this I was surprised. The Da I knew liked to know about everything that went on. He kept his ear down close to the ground. Forewarned is forearmed, I remember him telling me. That was back when he used to listen out for the storms coming across the scarlet plains. He liked to know about everything and it amazed me to hear that in the City he just didn't mind anymore. He hid himself away with Grandma, and hadn't even heard that his own children had arrived in town.

Anyhow. Never mind. They might have changed a little, but I still loved them. I put aside all my quibbles and small suspicions. I wrapped myself up tightly and descended the clanging, frosty metal stairs of the fire escape and hurried into the heart of the City.

2

All the way through Eventide District I could feel eyes on me. They were watching my every move.

I tried to shake them off by slipping down the narrowest of streets and taking random corners, but somehow they were always there. Just a few steps behind me. Someone was very interested in where I was going and what I might be up to.

I wasn't really paranoid. I knew I was completely sane about this. It was the Authorities. They were watching after me. They were dressing spies up as shoppers in the wintry streets and sending them after me. Bargain hunters in their scarves and long coats were peering at me and keeping tabs.

I made for the nearest Pipeline station. I was quite used to using the system now, buying my ticket at the clunky brass machine that emitted a blast of steam when it worked. Then through the turnstile and down the wooden escalator onto a green-tiled platform, slippery with melted snow. Waiting for the train I realised that this was the first time I'd been on my own for ages. In this crowd I could have been anyone at all. I could disappear amongst the mass of other people. Though, as my younger brother had pointed out before, I didn't look the same as they did. I looked too casual in my comfortable clothes. The City Insiders always looked so buttoned-up and formal: the men in their wingtip collars and the ladies in pinched waists and layers of dragging skirts. They looked like the Victorian British folk in my old electric novels, and I looked just like what I was: a peasant girl from the prairie. Tall and rangy. Not quite pretty, but not plain, either. I was hardy-looking and robust, Ma used to say, like you could plant me anywhere and I would grow. I'd never really been a girly-girl. Well, I didn't care.

There was a gust of warm wind, as the glowing oil lamps of the train appeared in the dark tunnel. It was at that very moment I felt those eyes upon me again. I turned quickly and this time I caught the culprit. There was a tall man looking at me. As the squeal of the train filled the tunnel he carefully placed his hand on my shoulder. No one but I could hear him giggling: '*Heeeee heeee heeeee…*'

The lights in the tunnel flickered and went off for a second. His grip tightened on my shoulder. Then, when the lightbulbs flashed on again he had vanished, but the train was there and the doors were opening. The whole crowd was surging forward and clambering aboard. I had to move quickly or I'd get left behind. I didn't want to be left alone on the platform.

All the way through the journey I sat in a crowded

compartment, stuffy with oily yellow smoke and a fug of overheated people. Did that man grasp my shoulder because I was standing too close to the edge of the platform and he was worried about me toppling over?

'*Heeee heee heeee…*'

No. I heard that giggling for real. I didn't imagine it. He was right by my side because he was following me. They were always following me. They knew where I was every minute of the day.

It was a relief to be out of the dingy, sooty tunnels of the Pipeline and in the open air once more. There was a fresh fall of snow coming down gently as I crossed the park into Stockpot District. Tall glass towers rose up everywhere, blocking the horizon. It all looked so much more gleaming and special than the shabbiness of where Da and Grandma lived. When they come to see me here, I thought, they'll be overawed by the sight of these green, monstrous buildings, stretching so high into the sky above.

And then, as I hurried through more bustling streets, I was thinking about the view I'd got on Christmas morning, of the whole City spread out below me. A magical view and a surprise Christmas present. I still felt like it could have been a dream, but I knew it wasn't. On Christmas morning, just a few short days ago, I flew over the tallest rooftops and chimneys and green domes and spires. I flew in the arms of one of my best and strangest friends … the Martian girl who I'd thought I might never see again. I didn't know why I had doubted her. Sook had a habit of turning up in my life…

Then, all at once, I was standing before the vast revolving doors of the building that had been my home ever since Al and I arrived in the City Inside. Downstairs, there was the usual busy market going on, with vendors crying out their wares and shoppers seething up and down the narrow walkways. There was a mass of colours and smells and noises: the hissing of oil on hotplates and the fiery spices the City people loved to cook with; the shiny metal of their fancy gadgets and brightly coloured gee-gaws everywhere. The City Insiders loved to be buying things and filling up their lives with all this stuff. I found it almost as bewildering as I did when I first explored this place, all those months ago.

But before I went up to my apartment there was someone I wanted to find.

I approached his usual pitch in the furthest corner of the market place, beyond the café which served the thickest, strongest coffee I had ever tasted. I could hear his music before I could see him. The soft, eerie notes from his miniature harp reached out to me through the crowd. Then, at last, I saw Peter, in his favourite red jumper with its holes and stretched-out sleeves. His music was even more doleful than usual. His messy, tangled strawberry blond hair hung down over his face so that I couldn't see his expression. I knew it'd be one of great concentration, his mouth pulling down at both corners as he focused on his song.

At his feet there was the case he carried his harp in. There were a few coins chucked in by passers-by. What lay next to it made my heart twinge with sadness. An old, hairy blanket. It was what Karl used to sleep on, day in day out, at Peter's feet. Of course it was quite empty now.

'Lora!' Peter cried out. He put down the harp and pushed his hair out of his face so he could see me better. His grin was like the winter clouds rolling away.

We hugged and I asked, 'No sign yet, huh?'

'I've been hanging out around Swiftnick's house. There's no way inside. It's like a castle.'

We knew the man who had taken Karl captive. We had watched, helplessly, as he carried Karl away in a cage. I didn't voice my deepest fear – that Dean Swiftnick had already murdered the little cat-dog, just out of spite. That wasn't what Peter wanted to hear.

He put on a bright and fake cheery grin. 'How was the rest of the holiday? Did you talk much with your da and grandma? I must send them a note to thank them for having me over on Christmas Day...'

He was gabbling away with too many questions. I wanted to sit down with a pot of strong brewed tea and talk properly. 'Come up to the apartment,' I told him. 'Can you leave your pitch for a while?'

'Yeah, it's not like I'm making a fortune today…'

As we shot up in the elevator through the innards of the grand building, I wondered about telling Peter how I suspected I was being watched down in the streets. I could still feel the impression left by that hand on my shoulder.

'You okay?' Peter asked.

I nodded and the lift glided to a halt at Storey 202.

Home again. I never imagined I'd think of that tidy high-up flat as my home. But it seemed like I'd become attached to it. I just wanted to sit there, all calmly, and gather my thoughts. I loved being with my family, but it turned out I loved my own space, too.

I took my key out of the new purse Da had given me for Christmas.

And the key wouldn't work in the lock.

Had it jammed? Was I doing it wrong?

I took out the key and tried again.

'What's up?' asked Peter.

'Someone's changed the locks … I've been locked out of my flat!'

It wasn't a mistake, I was sure. I'd been deliberately shut out of my home.

Peter noticed the letters slipped halfway under the door. I ripped them open and the first was from Al, dated a couple of days ago.

Lora, you never told me what you did at the university before Christmas. If you had I could have told you to expect this kind of thing. The Authorities don't like being messed around. I've learned that much from my time at *The City Insider*. When you promised them that you would go into the Remembering Machine and give up your memories for their university archive then you should've stuck to your word. You busted out of there and you caused damage to their expensive machines, is what I heard and the Dean of that department, Swiftnick, well he's a very important man, apparently. He's put in complaints about you with the Authorities and told them that you haven't been compliant and done what you ought to have done. So now they are making reprisals and punishing you. Now we're both homeless! Don't worry about me because the Graveley family say they will look after me and I can stay with them. They've been kind to me. But what about you, Lora? What will you do now? Your ever-loving brother, Alistair.

Peter read this rambling letter over my shoulder and we both gasped at the same bits.

'What's he doing staying with them?' Peter said.

'He should be with me,' I grimaced, folding the letter

back into its envelope. At the same time I was glad to learn he had a roof over his head, even if it was with the Graveleys.

The other letter had official stampings on and I didn't like the look of it at all.

'What's the other one?'

It was a bill. For rent arrears. For one of the best flats in the whole of Stockpot District, going back to the very day of our arrival in the City Inside, all those months ago.

Peter whistled and his eyebrows went so high they almost shot off his head. 'Two hundred thousand and ninety-two credits?'

'They can wait as long as they like for it,' I said. 'I ain't got nothing.'

Not even my belongings, I realised. The few bits and pieces of things I had picked up in the past year – just a few scraps of clothes and stuff, and my treasured belongings I had brought from Our Town – they were all gone. Either they were locked up in the apartment, or they'd been taken away, confiscated or dumped.

'What a mess,' said Peter. 'They've really got it in for you, haven't they?'

'I should have stayed in that memory machine and let them take my memories away,' I cursed myself. 'What do I need to remember for? What good will it do me?'

He shook his head. 'That machine wasn't stable. It was burning out your mind…'

He was right.

Now I needed to leave this fancy apartment block and let them stick their rent arrears where the Earth light don't shine.

I turned to go with Peter.

I didn't need more trouble, sure. But I seemed to find it wherever I went.

3

I was hardly aware of the journey we made back across town to the Den. Peter led the way, ushering me along. I was dawdling a bit, still a bit stunned, I guess, and feeling reluctant to leave behind the place that had been my home these past months.

Soon we were back on the Pipeline and getting out at Eventide District, passing through the frosty corridors of the neglected park with the fountains and the giant lizards. Everything was coated heavily with ice. If I'd been in a different mood I'd have loved to examine the spouts of water trapped in time and the shaggy layers of icicles mounting the stone dinosaurs. But not today.

Peter led us to the old bandstand and expertly felt around in the bleached ivy for the doorway that took us into the shrouded passageway and those tunnels lit by smudgy gas lamps. Down and down into the place that was more familiar to him than anywhere, but that filled me with a heavy kind of dread. It was a place that he swore existed beneath the radar of the Authorities, but I couldn't see how. Surely the rulers of the City Inside knew everything and everyone, and everywhere there was to hide?

'Thanks, Peter,' I mumbled, as we came to the cavernous interior of the Den, with its feeling of being a town square in the middle of all these buildings carved into the rock itself. He distracted me by telling me how this place was once above ground, many decades ago. A hideous space-plague had struck the population of this District – brought to Mars aboard one of the Celestial Omnibuses that secretly ferried people from planet Earth. The Authorities had stopped the spread of the plague by burying the entire district under huge amounts of rubble and dirt, trapping all the sick folk underground.

'That's horrible!' I gasped, as he told me this, later that day. We were both sitting on his bunk in the tiny alcove where he lived, in the scruffiest, least homely building there was in the Den. I wondered why he was telling me horror stories about the past like this? Was it to make me feel better about my horrible-looking future?

'Anyhow, loads of years went by and all that was left down here were some old skeletons and the space-plague had died out. After that us lot started using the place as a hideout. And it kind of grew and grew…'

We were eating our evening snack of pancakes with some kind of spicy meat in them. We'd bought them off a vendor in the gas-lit street outside. The fella seemed to know Peter, who was proud to introduce me as a new member of the Den. Well, I didn't want to be rude or nothing, but there was no way I was going to be living down there in that gloomy place. I didn't want to say as much to Peter outright, because he might have thought I was looking down on him. I wasn't – but I had more things to do than live in an old place like this. I had to find the rest of my family, for one.

But still, Peter was cheery that night because I was there, having a kind of sleepover in his alcove. He was so cheery he hadn't mentioned Karl once, though he did pause to lay out the little cat-dog's stinky rug at the foot of his bed.

We dozed on his bunk. We even hugged close at one point in the night. We were both in our clothes and I didn't for a moment think that Peter would get any funny ideas. He was acting like a brother towards me, like he always had. You'd have had to be crazy to think there could be anything romantic going on between us. Neither of us was that kind of person, to be honest.

Once in the night, when we were both awake, I found myself describing Sook to him, and how Sook came to me in the very early hours of Christmas morning. And that miraculous flight we took through the empty skies and I could see all the domes and spires of the City Inside.

'Wow, Lora. I dunno if I'm dreaming now or you were dreaming then. It all sounds a bit strange. Are you really sure?'

I nodded and smiled. The place was steeped in inky shadows. The whole dormitory around us was mostly still. Beds creaked further away. There was the sound of snuffling, breathing, snoring. The people all around us sounded like an attic filled with lizard birds, snoozing in the rafters. I decided to tell Peter more about Sook and my history with her. How I'd known her for some time. How she came to me, way back when we lived in the Homestead, and how she took me on these magical flights. And how she had kept coming back, every now and then, as our journey went on through the wilderness.

'A real live Martian girl!' Peter could hardly believe it. 'But wasn't she dangerous, Lora? If the ghosts were … eating folk and … and…'

'Sometimes she said weird stuff, about all that,' I admitted. 'Sometimes I was frightened by the things she said. But at the same time, I knew she was my friend, too. She would never hurt me. She used to come and warn me and help us. I knew I was safe when we flew together.'

Peter listened in silence. He thought over what I'd said for ages. Then he was asking what Sook looked like, and about her wings. He wanted to know everything I could tell him about her Martian people and where they came from, where they lived. And what they were doing Disappearing folk away.

'I don't know,' I said. 'I don't know about the Disappearances at all now. I'd assumed that people were taken away, never to be seen again … and that was horrible, but … you could kind of understand it. But now I know they come back, don't I?' He took hold of my hand in the dark and squeezed it. 'My da and grandma. They just turned up again, here. Almost exactly the same as they were before, before the Martians took them. I just can't figure it out, Peter.'

'But don't they have anything to say about it?' he asked. 'Didn't you ask them, over Christmas? About where they had been? How they got here?'

'I tried. But they wouldn't really answer. I don't think they really know…'

We both thought about this for a while. Peter was making me consider things I didn't really want to. Big questions I'd pushed away while Christmas was going on.

'I don't like it,' Peter said at last. 'There's something horrible in this.'

Our voices must have got louder as we talked, because some gruff-sounding guy from another alcove yelled at us then. 'You oughta hush your racket! You shouldn't be in our Den anyway! You oughta get outa here!'

I'm not sure I belonged anywhere anymore.

Next day I wound up having a row with Grandma.

She was crazy again. I could hear it in her voice and see the look in her eyes. Soon as I got back into that flat at the top of the building hidden away behind the department store. Soon as I stepped indoors I could tell by her glowering face she had something to ask me. She clearly wasn't happy.

'Toaster,' she said. 'Where's Toaster gone?'

Over Christmas I'd avoided this question. The reason was because I just didn't know. He was away having repairs done, somewhere at the university. He'd gone off voluntarily to have his memory looked at and repaired. He knew there was stuff he wasn't recalling properly and he gave himself up to be examined. But since he went there'd been no word and now, I realised, with my eviction from the apartment, he wouldn't know where to go or how to find me again. There was a danger that we could become separated in the City Inside. The thought filled me with dismay all over again.

Grandma looked like she was panicking, too. 'I know he was with you. He came with you to the City. He looked after you and Al just like he did me all my life. And now you're telling me that you lost that robot? You just lost track of him somehow?'

I tried to reason with Grandma and explain what had happened. I tried to tell her that in recent times Toaster seemed to have had more of a mind of his own than before. He was making his own decisions and going off more, meeting in the laundry room with friends he made amongst the other Servo-Furnishings who worked in our building. I even recall him saying that he was off to special gatherings, like there were groups that Servos were organising together. It was all kind of mysterious and, now I thought about it, he was getting to have a kind of attitude about him.

Grandma lost her temper. She wasn't following anything I was saying. She was midway through taking down the Christmas decorations, unwinding twists of dusty tinsel and dropping them on the carpet. She yanked down the flimsy paper chains and ripped them into shreds. Everything looked bleak in the daylight that came through the blinds. Soon Grandma was smashing stuff up. Flinging down the glass ornaments and grinding them under her heels. She was surprisingly strong, even though she was old and beat up. This was just like in the past, when she'd go crazy and fling stuff about. I knew it was no good yelling at her and trying to make her calm down. It just made her worse.

Luckily Da came in, not too long after that. By then Grandma had worn herself out, trashing the living room. I'd holed up in the tiny kitchen, which was a bit less messy and dirty than it had been the day before. I heard Da treat Grandma kindly, and not get too angry about the stuff she'd wrecked. He led her away to her bedroom and gave her pills to knock her out for a while, until the madness had passed. I could still hear her yammering on: 'That girl knows where Toaster is! She sent him away! She wanted his memory cracked open! She wanted to know everything, like they always do. They always want to know everything that old sunbed can't forget…'

'Hush, hush, Ma,' he said. Eventually she hushed up her howling.

Da came back and I stepped out of the kitchen and we both stood in the multi-coloured wreckage of Christmas.

'I've been chucked out of the apartment by the Authorities,' I told him. 'So has Al, but he's already got somewhere to live. The Graveleys have taken him in.'

Da raised an eyebrow. 'The Graveleys?'

'They think a lot of him,' was all I said for now. 'They reckon he has a future at the paper and all.'

'I see,' said Da. 'It must have been awful for you. Going back and finding out.'

'It was.' I didn't say anything about Al's note and its almost gloating tone. 'It's because I wouldn't do what they wanted. Go in the Remembering Machine and all. Grandma thinks I should just have done what they told me…'

Da shrugs. 'You've got to do what your conscience tells you. I always taught you that.'

'I didn't want to give them all our years on the prairie and the years before that. My memories are precious to me.'

Da nodded. But he didn't look like he exactly agreed with me. This was surprising. I'd have expected him to think just the same as me. Weren't those years out there in the wilderness precious to him too?

'Sometimes the fight just goes out of you,' he explained, as we set about clearing up the mess.

'Can I live here? With you?'

'Of course,' he said. 'There'll always be a place for you.'

'You don't really have the room.'

'You stay here with me and your grandma,' he told me firmly. 'She isn't always insane, as you know. She'll be pleased you're coming home to us.'

We lifted the pine tree, which was shedding dried-out needles all over the carpet. 'Let's haul this thing down to the alley,' he said. 'And I can tell you about the brilliant idea I just had.'

'What brilliant idea?'

He tapped his nose and grinned and together we hoisted the dead tree into the hallway and into the cold outside. 'An idea about how you can pay your way. I'm gonna get you a little job, Lora. So you won't have idle hours sitting here.'

'What kind of job?'

'Just wait.' He looked so pleased with himself. 'Do you by any chance remember that old hobo from Our Town, Old Man Horace? The first one who Disappeared?'

4

Remember me telling you how the Disappearances happened in Our Town? Well, no one was really bothered at first. They'd just whisper and mutter about how a family lost their baby because it flew out of the window and never came back. Or how the town's old mascot tramp was last seen heading out of town and after a few days people were realising he'd never come back.

Well, here I was standing face to face with that old hobo who Disappeared. Old Man Horace, we always called him and I had assumed he was gone for good. But here he was in the City Inside, working at the selfsame place my da was working. And he was just as stinky and ragged as ever but for some reason I found myself almost crying when I saw him again. I even hugged him.

His bristly old beard scratched just the same and he was still wearing the same lopsided hat with the broad brim. All of a sudden I was transported back to our house when he came to stay for Christmas a couple of times, and a Martian Thanksgiving.

When I asked him, 'What are you doing here?' he took the question literally and started to show me the stuff he was working on. He was making toys. He and Da were working in a toy workshop. It was a cellar deep under one of the tenements, dimly lit with oil lamps and kept warm by an old pot-bellied stove. There were workbenches and hand tools lying amongst pale wood shavings. And now that I looked I saw there were shelves all over the walls. On each of them were small, marvellously carved figurines. Men, women, lizards.

I remembered that this was what he'd do when we were little. Having no money at all for presents for the folks he stayed with, Old Man Horace whittled hunks of old wood into wonderful shapes. I'd kept the smooth, gnarled toys he'd made for me until the very day we had to flee the Homestead. And here he was, still doing the same kind of magic work.

'He won't believe it,' Da chuckled. 'But his toys are selling very well indeed, up above ground. In the fancy stores and toyshops of the City Inside.'

Yes! I realised, with a shock. I had seen them. I was in one of those sophisticated stores, right before Christmas with Al. We were both amazed and disturbed by the wooden toys we saw. They appeared to be models of our old farmhouse, populated by tiny carved replicas of ourselves, our parents, even our burden beasts. We couldn't understand how that could be – we had no idea that Da and Old Man Horace were here. With a flush of shame I remembered how I had pocketed the carved figure of the mother, filching her out of her kitchen and popping her into my pocket. Well, now I knew how those toys came about, and how they were so accurate.

'I make the buildings,' said Da, looking proud. 'I built the originals, didn't I? It's easy, putting together tiny versions. Working on these toys – well, it's like we're keeping our old lives still alive somehow. That's how both Horace and I feel, ain't it?'

Old Man Horace nodded enthusiastically. It's then I realised that he hadn't said a word yet. He started up making these rough, choking noises in his throat and Da got up and patted his arm. 'You don't have to try to speak, Horace. Relax. I know it's painful. Take a drink.'

The old man produced a bottle of some strong kind of potion from his jacket pocket. It smelled a bit like medicine, a bit like moonshine.

'He finds it difficult to talk nowadays,' Da told me. 'Some kind of accident he had between leaving Our Town and winding up here. I don't know all the details of what happened, but I think he was injured and never got it stitched up or seen to properly. He was living on the streets here in the City when I saw him again…'

'That must have been so scary for him…' It was bad enough for me, adjusting to the City Inside, and I had the company of my brother and our sunbed, and we were in a luxury apartment. How much more terrifying must it have been for Old Man Horace?

I was still thinking about this later that morning, when Da set me to brushing up all the shavings and stuff from the floor.

'You're doing good work. We desperately need this place cleaning up. It's a safety hazard, you see. And Horace and I have got to keep working now there's all these orders coming in. We can't let up for a moment…'

'It's great that you've both made a success of this,' I told him.

He shrugged. 'It's something to do. We still need to eat.'

I looked at him and once more it was like the fight had gone out of my da. He was smaller somehow. Shrunken up. Also, in recent days, he'd stopped concealing various things from me – the way he limped so badly, and got out of breath so quickly. He had been injured lastingly and he'd been trying to hide it. I went cold inside, remembering how, the last time I'd seen him, on the day he Disappeared, the hovercart had dropped on him, crushing his ribs and organs, making blood bubble up in his mouth. He was so lucky to be alive, I realised.

'You haven't told me much about the Martian Ghosts,' I said. 'Did they speak to you? Did they tell you anything? Did they explain why they were bringing you here?'

A whole range of expressions rushed across his face. They were hard to read because the smoky light in the cellar workroom was so bad away from the benches. Was he reluctant to talk to me about this? What happened to him after he was taken away?

'I haven't said much because it doesn't matter now,' Da said. 'All that is over. We Disappeared and then they brought us here. They didn't treat us badly. Not really. We never understood what was going on and that was scary for a while. But I do believe, Lora, and you must believe me when I tell you this. I do believe that the Martian Ghosts mean us no harm. I don't think they ever did.'

It was the first time I'd ever heard him say anything like that. And I was glad, because that was what I had come to believe, too.

We were eating our late supper that night and then without warning someone was knocking at the front door. It was a knocking full of authority. Like whoever it was had a perfect right to be there. Someone who never wondered if they were in the right place.

'What a horribly chilly evening, may we come in? What an extraordinary place you're living in. Wonderful, really. How quaint this District is.'

When Da opened the door I heard the voice talking from the other end of the hall and a chill ran through me. I knew those cultivated tones and that way of assuming that everyone was going to do as he said.

'Help, Lora, quick!' gasped Grandma, jumping up from the supper table. 'Help me clear up our mess…'

'But we're still eating,' I protested.

'We mustn't let people come in and see us eating,' she gasped. 'Not strangers. Not polite company. Here, carry these dishes...'

And so we were dashing about, trying to make the place look more respectable, when Mr Graveley entered the room. He was wearing his long black coat with the fur collar again, and a tall hat that seemed to brush the ceiling. He looked about the living room and his eyes were the brightest things in the whole place. They lit upon me and he smiled nastily. I opened my mouth to say something but it was like he had sucked all the oxygen out of my lungs just by standing there.

'Lora, dear,' he nodded. 'How are you?'

'Answer the gentleman!' croaked Grandma, jabbing me with her tea towel. Then she stood before Graveley and actually curtsied. Like he was the king in one of the old video dramas she used to like to watch. Something from old Earth. She was showing off her knowledge of how to treat Very Important Folk and Mr Tollund Graveley actually purred with pleasure.

'And you must be the famous Margaret Estelle Robinson,' said the tall dark man from the other side of the City. The powerful man who owned the newspaper and who was thick with the Authorities. The man who seemed to control all our lives in his own careful, underhand way.

Grandma's eyes – one real and one glass – almost popped out when she heard him speak her name. 'Y-you know me?'

'Of course, naturally,' and here he gave an elaborate bow. 'Allow me to make the acquaintance of one of the first settlers in the wilderness. You are a legend, madam.'

She went all coy. 'Oh, really. Well, I never did.' She was hideously girlish, all of a sudden. There were sparks firing off her clunky metal leg as she stood there in front of him but she hardly even noticed.

Just then I realised who was with Mr Graveley. Not just some lackey in a fancy suit. It was my brother, looking all grown up and smart. I'd never seen him so mature and handsome-looking. Unfortunately he was with that simpering idiot girl of his, Tillian, who was strapped up in all her finery again. She wasn't as good at keeping a straight poker face as her da. She looked around at the apartment with undisguised scorn. I guess it all looked pretty poor and pathetic compared with the luxury she was used to.

'Al?' Da asked, stepping into the living room. 'Are you going to introduce us to this young lady, and this gentleman?' In his own quiet, gruff way, Da was letting the interlopers know that he was in charge here, while they were under his humble roof.

Looking embarrassed, Al made the necessary introductions. I watched as Da studied the Graveley father and daughter. He shook Mr Graveley's hand and I could tell he wasn't impressed. He wouldn't trust that man a single inch.

Grandma however was just about piddling herself with excitement.

'Da,' said Al nervously. 'Tillian is my ... my fiancée. We intend to marry this summer.'

Da's eyes widened.

'It might seem to you that the children are rather young,' Tollund Graveley said smoothly. 'But I assure you, sir, that their courting and their nuptial plans are nothing out of the ordinary here in the City Inside. Certainly, in the upper tier of society – where we belong – such arrangements are not unusual.'

'I see,' said Da. 'We belong to the upper tier, do we?'

'*We* do,' said Graveley. 'And that's all that matters. My family will of necessity draw yours into our orbit and elevate you and your standing.' He looked ever so pleased with himself as he said this.

'Oh, listen, Edward!' cried Grandma. 'Oh, please say it's true! We're going up in the world at last! We're going back up to where we belong! After years and years of going down and down and down and down and living in poverty and danger...'

Da shot his mother a dark look as she said all of this. Mr Graveley and his daughter were simply amused by Grandma's reaction. She was practically dancing a jig. I realised she was still standing there with a gravy boat and a tea cloth.

Mr Tollund Graveley chuckled quietly under his breath. But I could hear his soft laughter. '*Heeee heeeee heeee heeeee…*'

And his daughter was laughing at Grandma's excitement, too. '*Heee heee heee*!'

Grandma went and hugged Al to her old-lady bosom, and ruffled up his immaculate hair. 'We're going up in the world! At last! At last! No more scraping a living for us! No more scritching and scratching for us!'

Al didn't say anything at all. He was even quieter than I was. I wondered, shouldn't he be all happy and crowing like Grandma? If it's really what he wants?

Just then Mr Graveley produced a gold-edged invitation card from deep within the long dark coat he wore.

'Something else. I brought this to you. I thought I'd deliver it in person. It's the New Year Ball at the Planetarium. All the great and the good will be there. Everyone who counts. We'll all be attending. I hope your family will join us on Saturday night? The elite of the City Inside would love to meet you…'

5

Even though he couldn't talk much any more, Old Man Horace could still communicate fine. He wrote in flowing, decorative handwriting on sheets of paper and when he had something important to say at work he would pass one of these notes along the bench to me or Da. Mostly he sat there carving into hunks of soft wood, making his tiny replicas of Ma and Toaster, Molly and George and the rest of us. Mostly his notes were to do with work, orders and supplies, but when Da was out of the way on an errand he would talk about more important things.

'Your da is heartbroke,' one note said, about this time. 'It ain't just in his body that's been broke up and injured. His heart's been surely broke, too. Your coming back to him, and your brother Al, that has restored some life to him. But it still weighs heavy on him that he is away from your mom and your sister. The months are going by and they're turning into years and he feels so helpless…'

I read this, and I knew that Horace was telling the truth. He seemed to know my da better than anyone. He was his oldest friend, really. Da hadn't talked much to me about Ma and Hannah. I knew that was 'cause it hurt too much. When he tried to do so a lost look came over his face. He didn't know how to begin to look for them. His letters to the Authorities came back unopened.

Following Mr Tollund Graveley's surprise appearance in the apartment, Da had been kicking himself. 'I just went dumb, didn't I?' he growled, a couple of nights later. We were at the supper table and Da was being unusually candid with his thoughts. 'Graveley is powerful. He knows things. He's connected to the Authorities, to everyone. He could find out anything…'

'What are you going on about, Edward?' shouted Grandma. 'I don't understand why you're looking so upset all the time. Didn't you hear the man? We're going to a glamorous party! And our little Alistair is marrying into a wealthy family! Good times, Edward! Our just rewards!'

Da just shook his head at her. 'I'm talking about my wife. My daughter. The rest of our family. Graveley could help us, maybe, to find them…'

I was shocked at the dismissive wave of her hand Grandma gave at his words. But I knew, too, how difficult it would be to find our folks. I knew how huge the planet was. Far better than my elders did. I just kept quiet over supper. My hand in my pocket closed around the wooden figurine of Ma that I had taken to carrying around everywhere.

'Graveley wants something from us,' Da was saying. 'He

wants his daughter to marry Al. But I sense there's something more he wants or needs from us, just from the way he was being so nicey-nice…'

'Yes!' I broke in. 'He's a slimeball, Da. He was at the university when they were trying to steal my memories. He was part of it all, he…'

Grandma rose to her feet and her face was thunderous. 'Don't you go spoiling this, girly, with all your shenanigans! You already been causing enough fuss for the grown-ups to sort out. I won't let you spoil this. We have a wonderful chance to better ourselves at last! To reclaim our heritage as settlers and people of note. Don't you go meddling!'

It was a long speech from Grandma who, let's face it, usually expressed herself by throwing furniture about. Both Da and I watched her stomp off to her room.

'She has trouble understanding stuff these days,' Da sighed. 'All she knows is that some important man has promised to take her to a big party. She's reliving her youth now, and thinking she can go back to being that girl who was somebody because she was going to Mars…'

Later that night I was thinking about how Grandma was so excited about being important again and how she was so different from Da and me. All we wanted was to live out happy, quiet lives where we wouldn't bother anyone and no one would bother us. We were both kind of wary of the popularity of the Martian Homestead playsets and figurines. It felt like giving too much of ourselves away. But the toys were more popular than ever, said the company who handled the orders, and there was no choice but to carry on making them.

I sat by the window in the living room in my night things, long after Da and Grandma had retired for the night. I was about to roll out my bedding on the floor but first I was looking up at the Earth light shining blue and misty through the layers of smoky fug that surrounded the City Inside like a protective dome. The sky was a little clearer than usual tonight, and I was hoping, without even realising it, that I would see a small figure up there, dancing through the heavens on those long, elaborate, chocolate and indigo moth-like wings of hers. I was hoping to see Sook again, and that she was keeping a good watch over us all.

Later in the week I took another look at the invitation Mr Graveley had given us and realised I was going to need a date. They were keen that everyone attended going in two by two, in pairs of males and females, all formally attired. Grandma informed me with glee that this would mean my wearing a ball gown of some description. Instinctively my gut recoiled at this. Once only in my life had I been forced to wear a real girly-girl dress like that. A hideous silken thing that Grandma and her lifelong friend Ruby were insisting on buying for me, back in Our Town. I was so sickened by the experience that I vomited profusely in Madame Lucille's swanky boutique and was hounded out of there right away. They forced me to wash out that horrid frock in Ruby's old stone sink.

Da looked solemn. 'Your grandma's right, I'm afraid, Lora. If we want to go to this thing – and we have to – then we gotta play by their crazy rules. Look at me, I gotta find a dinner suit. How am I gonna find one I can afford?'

But Grandma had been doing a bit of research in the local stores and she'd gotten wind of a clean, respectable place that would loan you fancy get-ups or anything you needed and charged you by the hour. The rates were good, the garments were clean. It wasn't too far away.

I still felt kind of mutinous. 'Well, I'll come and take a look. But nothing too dumb-looking. And also, I'll only come along if Peter can be my date.'

They had no problem with that. They'd both liked Peter when he came to stay at Christmas. And why not? He was a polite, handsome boy, who always seemed to know just the right thing to say. Better than I ever did. Yeah, they had liked him a lot.

'Huh, what's this?' crowed Grandma. 'He gonna be your date, is he? Is there something we should know about, Lora girl? Maybe Al and Tillian ain't the only sweethearts in this family right now, eh?'

I shuddered at the way she was teasing and carrying on. I snapped back at her, because she was getting on my nerves. 'Peter ain't like that. He ain't interested in me like that. And it's just as well because we're only pals.'

Da looked at me, frowning, 'Every boy is like that, Lora. You can't be naive. Every boy is after one thing in the end, specially the age Peter's at.'

I shook my head firmly. 'No, sir. Peter ain't like that cause Peter don't really like girls. Not in that way. He likes boys, see.' A little of my own disappointment at this fact came blurting out of me as I said it.

And I knew I'd gone too far right away because of the way Da and Grandma were staring at me.

'He what?' Grandma squawked.

Da was concerned. He got a sorry look on his face. 'Lora, I don't want you getting mixed up with criminals and such...'

'He ain't no criminal,' I shrugged off their serious looks.

'That boy,' gasped Grandma. 'I thought he was sweet. Turns out too sweet, huh? It's his mother I feel sorry for. She got a wrong 'un. A defective one.'

'He doesn't see his mother or his family,' I told them. 'He don't live with them...' I was saying too much, but I couldn't stop myself.

'Lora, maybe you'd better find yourself another date for the ball,' suggested my da. 'We don't want no trouble. What about Horace?'

I stood my ground. 'You'd rather I took some drunk old guy who used to sleep in the street?' And immediately I felt bad for saying this about Horace, who had never been anything but kind to me.

'I think we should all calm down,' said Da.

'I ain't going to no ball with a fancy-nancy boy in tow,' Grandma growled.

'Ma, that's enough,' Da said tersely. 'There's no need for that. You can't tell from looking what Peter really is. Providing he don't show us up, I don't see why we shouldn't take him along with us.'

I headed out in the evening to visit the secret Den, in order to tell Peter what we'd been discussing. I felt guilty all the way through the still-frozen streets. Now the sales were on in the glitzy stores there were more people coming and going than ever, and I was having to shove my way through the window shoppers.

Would Peter mind that I'd given away his secrets to my family? What was I thinking of? He spent his whole life being so careful. He stayed in that gloomy Den under the park, taking such care to make sure no one knew where he lived. He trusted me with the knowledge of how to get there. It maybe was a bit grim down there, but it was better than the places the Authorities sent you if they knew you didn't dance to the tune they wanted. Where they scrambled your mind and turned you upside down and before you knew it, you were someone else entirely.

I had played fast and loose with Peter's secret. Maybe I didn't need to tell him what I'd done?

My stream of thoughts was interrupted as I caught a glimpse of something out of the corner of my eye...

I was outside the biggest of the department stores. It had the tallest, brightest windows. The frosty glimmer of its displays even penetrated the yellowish fog that was choking Bolingbroke District that night. I'd glanced at a display of toys and smiled with satisfaction to see our Martian Homestead in pride of place. But when I looked that way, there was a man standing by the window and he grinned back at me. A bland, stupid-looking grin.

And suddenly he was standing right beside me. How did he move so fast?

I bolted and started to run. But then he had me by the arm. Both his hands were clamped about my left wrist and he was digging in his nails.

'Stay here,' he told me. His voice had a high-pitched quality to it. He was wearing a hat that covered his face with shadow. His knotted scarf had white and blood red stripes. 'I've got you, Lora. We're watching you, Lora. We see you everywhere you go.'

'Get off me...' my voice came out low and hollow, my words all slowed down. All around the crowds were parting and going around us and no one seemed to notice that this man – this creature – was holding me captive.

'Don't panic, don't wriggle, Lora,' he said. He glanced

over his dark glasses at me and I saw that his eyes were purple and they were starting to spiral round. '*Heee heee heee...*'

'What do you want from me?' I burst out at him.

'We want to learn all we can from you, Lora,' he said sternly. 'All we want to do is wring out your mind. You must let us learn from you. There are things that we must know...'

It felt like I was falling under the swirly spell of his eyes, but then I managed to wrest myself free of his damp grasp. I swung round and ran from him as fast as I could, never letting up or looking back for a second until I reached the park and the Den.

6

Soon enough it was Saturday.

Strange how, when it was something she wanted, Grandma could be so together and organised. She took us down the old costume hire place she had found, getting us all gussied up.

But maybe I was being too awful about Grandma. I'd forgotten how her moods could go up and down so sharply. I was seeing only the negative sides of the old lady, and forgetting how sweet and lovely she could be. When it came to paying for these expensive dress-hirings and trips in fancy cars, she opened up her secret savings and spent them without hesitation. Da and I felt foolish in our fancy outfits, but it did kinda feel nice to have Grandma admiring us and saying what a picture we looked.

Peter, too. Even after the awful things she had called him just the other day, she welcomed him warmly and encouraged him to choose a smart suit from the dressy-up place that he'd feel comfortable in. Of course, he looked like a prince in midnight blue velvet and a purple waistcoat. We all admired him out loud. And they all turned and applauded me, and managed not to snigger at the dress I forced myself into. It was plain but you could see it was sophisticated, the colour of buttermilk and cut very finely so it showed off what Grandma described as my 'beautiful new figure'. Huh.

And Da looked about twenty years younger, beard and hair trimmed, immaculate in a dust-red suit. 'Like on the picture from your wedding day,' Grandma choked up. 'You've not aged a day, Edward.'

'That ain't true,' he said quietly, and I knew he was thinking of Ma, and how she should be with us.

Grandma vanished for a while and came back attired in a backless, strapless black dress that squeezed her tight as a roast as it comes spitting hot fat from the oven. She had ruffles everywhere and her face was painted as garish as a sunset in the rainy season. None of us had ever seen her done up like this and we all said how amazing she looked. She took our compliments nicely, never suspecting for a moment that we'd all had to lie a bit. I wondered what the fancy folk at the ball would think of her, all painted up like that?

Yet I needn't have worried. Grandma somehow knew more about the way people dressed in the City Inside than I did. She'd been round the department stores and she'd looked at the newspapers and come to the conclusion that you had to wear a whole lot of make-up and that bright, flashy colours were the fashion of the day. When we turned up at the Planetarium in the expensive wagon she'd hired we were struck dumb by the fact that these rich people all looked as overdone and clown-like as Grandma.

The journey across town was thrilling. New snow had fallen, giving a smooth and easy glide to the covered sleigh that was transporting us. Two tall lizards were pulling the sled, elegant beasts who weren't at all put off by the traffic and the flashing lights of the City. The four of us sat up back sipping from the steaming flasks that our driver had given us before setting off. He'd also offered rugs to put over our knees and so we were pretty cosy, sliding through the snowy City streets, sipping this spicy hot cocktail and feeling like we were somebodies at last.

Grandma was in her element. Even more so, when we arrived in Ruskin District, at the very heart of the City. Our sleigh came to a halt in front of the largest, grandest building any of us had yet seen. The Planetarium was a vast, green-domed building and it was towards its ornate doors that the City's most important citizens were flocking that night.

A small orchestra was arranged outside the front entrance, all togged up against the cold, playing tunes that had, during my few months in the City, already become familiar to me. All around us, as we shuffled up the snowy pink carpet, careful not to slip in our new, unfamiliar shoes, flashbulbs were going off. Faces were peering at us from the crowds that lined the streets and walkways. Everyone seemed keen to know who we were, and why we'd been invited to the party of the year. We tried to behave like the other guests. They were putting their noses in the air and ignoring all the interest and the flashing cameras. They just glided smoothly towards the Planetarium and behaved like they couldn't hear a thing.

'Wow,' Peter kept shaking his head. 'I've never seen anything like this. Only in the papers…'

I remembered how Peter had said that, ever since he was thrown out of university, he'd spent part of almost every day reading in the City Library, getting himself an education. I imagined him staring at black and white images of the Annual Planetarium Ball and picturing himself here.

I was concentrating on walking in heels and trying to feel natural in my dress. The material was so flimsy though, I felt like I was dressed in my night-clothes; everything felt peculiar and dreamlike.

The orchestra played louder and soon we could hear a gentle hubbub from inside the domed building. It built and built until we passed through those tall, carved doors and into the marble hallway beyond. The noise inside was tremendous and echoing – every little murmur and chuckle from the many hundreds of guests seemed amplified hugely, all the echoes bouncing around the stone dome. Another orchestra struck up a series of jaunty tunes and this was better than all that excited chatter, but I still thought our ears would be ringing for days to come.

Our small party stuck together. We tottered through a crowd of folk who seemed to feel confident about belonging there. The air was hot with the mingled scents of booze and cologne. You could get high just by breathing too deeply in that room, I thought. Da led the way, deeper and deeper into the crush and, just when I was starting to wonder what it was he was looking for, or where he was heading, he stopped and told us all to look up.

'Huh? Say what?' croaked Grandma. She had acquired a plateful of crumbly snacks and was feeding herself greedily. She looked up as ordered by Da. We all did and we all gave a gasp of pleasant surprise.

Of course, we should have guessed. The place was a Planetarium, it said so on our invitation, and on the signs outside the building. I had flown right over its huge green dome with Sook, but I hadn't really considered what must be inside.

The dark was crammed full with what seemed like all of the heavens. Luminous globes of sky-scarlet and Earthly blue waltzed about each other and heliotrope moons fussed nimbly in orbits of their own. A weighty golden world swung stately hula hoops about her waist and comets went off like fireworks in clattering celebration.

'It's the whole universe in miniature,' sobbed Grandma. She had a vol-au-vent raised to her mouth and her rapture was so intense she simply dropped it on the floor. 'Oh, Edward. It's so beautiful. It's how I remember it all, from the portals. I spent so many hours staring out of the *Melville*'s windows and it all looked like this. Looking outside every day and night. Space was so beautiful. I think I'd forgotten how wonderful it was…' Then she fell silent, staring upwards, tears making a hash of her fashionable make-up.

Peter reached for my hand and squeezed it. 'I've never been in here before,' he whispered. 'They don't let in common rabble. Thank you. Thanks for inviting me,' he added.

I looked at the other partygoers. Hardly any were looking up. They were more interested in checking out who else had been invited, what they were wearing and how each other looked. They didn't look up at the shining galaxy over our heads, I realised, because they felt they had seen it all before.

After a while we began to get used to the push and the crush of the party, without feeling too claustrophobic or panicky about not really belonging. 'We're as good as anyone else here, Lora,' Da told me, grinning. 'Look at us in our fancy get-ups! Is there a family here as handsome as us?' He was eating sticky ribs and drinking some kind of foaming beer and I saw him talking to a couple of complete strangers. Then I remembered how, back in our old lives, Da had always enjoyed being at parties. He used to love playing host when we had neighbourly barbecues.

'Look at this lot,' Peter said thoughtfully at one point. 'If someone dropped a bomb on this place right now, then the City Inside would be without all its leaders and everyone who thinks of themselves as important.'

I looked around, but I didn't know any of the faces. With his knowledge of politics and public life, Peter could reel off names easy as anything. He pointed out ministers and priests and writers and famous actors and seemed almost as excited as Grandma when he recognised certain individuals.

Then all of a sudden we saw a family more handsome than even ourselves. Peter noticed them first. They were moving through the crowd at a stately pace, almost as if they were royalty. It was the Graveley family, just Ma and Pa, their drippy daughter and our Al in tow, but the way folk drew back to admire them and pay compliments you'd have thought it was a whole cavalcade coming through.

'Your brother brushes up well,' Peter observed.

I stared at the Graveleys critically. Al had his hair smarmed down and they'd put some kind of powder and pink blush on his face, as seemed to be the modish thing for young gentlemen in the City this season. He looked proper hoity-toity, I thought as he dogged the elegant footsteps of his future in-laws. His bride-to-be looked just ridiculous, I thought. She had a kind of basket on her head, no lie. It was woven out of silver wire and decorated with stuffed dead birds and miniature roses. Her frock was equally outrageous and conspicuously expensive. Its enormous size was another reason everyone had to draw back in order to let the Graveley family pass through.

'Crikey O'Riley!' Grandma cried out, when she saw this display. Then she was beaming with pride and turning to strangers beside us, telling them, 'That's my grandson, you know. We're so proud he's made something of himself.'

I saw those strangers give her vinegary smiles and back away from her. But still they seemed envious and admiring of the Graveleys as they swept through the hall.

Then they were gone. They'd passed right by us without even noticing or realising we were there.

'Hey!' Grandma shouted after them. 'Hey, what the hell? You too good for us now?'

'Hush, Ma,' Da told her, and gently took her arm. The orchestra struck up an exceedingly old tune from Earth and he led her out to a space on the floor. Grandma stood half as tall as her son, and he'd lost some of his skill for dancing, but they still looked a picture and my heart caught in my throat as I watched them.

But Peter was watching elsewhere.

He nudged me and said something in a voice so unusual, so filled with anger, that I didn't quite work out it was him speaking at first.

He said: 'Dean Swiftnick is over there.'

And sure enough, looking very elegant in his evening dress, the boss of the university was standing across the dance floor, watching the crowd with shrewd eyes. My blood ran cold at the sight of the man who'd wanted to drain my mind in that horrible machine of his.

Then Peter's voice changed. He cried out in surprise and excitement: 'Lora! Look who he's got with him!'

I blinked hard and at first I couldn't tell under the shifting lights of the fake stars and planets who it was that Peter meant.

But when I saw I couldn't believe my eyes.

7

The smarmy professor was all togged up in a cape and a hat and he had a twirly moustache under his pointed nose, so that he looked even more like a villain from an old book. Next to him hovered a flying disc kind of thing, and on top of that rested the small, very familiar form that had grabbed Peter's attention and rendered him speechless.

It was Karl, the kidnapped cat-dog, sitting on the floating disc, and tethered to Dean Swiftnick by a fancy collar and chain. Karl looked healthier than he had for quite some time, but he looked bothered by the noise of the party, and he was covering his small face with his paws.

'Karl!' Peter burst out, and in about three strides he was over there.

'Peter…!' I tried to grab his coat tails, thinking that it probably wasn't the best approach, to go storming in.

'Ah, look who it is,' purred the man who had tried to steal the contents of my mind. 'Peter and Lora. How are you, you two naughty children. Hm?'

'You've got him,' said Peter, sounding choked up. He turned away from both the old professor and me and started fussing over Karl, putting both arms around him. The small creature started yapping and squirming at once.

'Oh, dear, you've startled him, my boy,' tutted Swiftnick. 'He's a very sensitive creature.'

Peter was appalled. Karl's hackles were up and he was snarling at the boy who had looked after him for so many years. 'Karl? What's wrong? You remember me, don't you?'

'I shouldn't be surprised if he hasn't forgotten all about you, dear boy,' chuckled Swiftnick. He stopped a waitress and made her stand by him as he emptied her tray of canapés, stuffing them into his mouth one by one. 'Karl has been living in the lap of luxury ever since I rescued him. The poor creature was in a terrible state. I shouldn't be at all surprised if he wouldn't rather forget his whole, terrible, previous, hand-to-mouth existence with you…'

This made me see red. I knew how much Peter and Karl loved and depended upon each other. 'You're enjoying this,' I snarled at Swiftnick.

Peter was still concentrating on his beloved pet, trying to calm him down. But Karl backed away and bared his tiny fangs. It was then I realised that his usually tangled and malformed legs were straighter than before. They were just the same shape as any other four-legged creature's. But they were cybernetic.

'What have you done to him?' Peter demanded.

'We had his little limbs repaired,' Swiftnick said smugly. 'He isn't quite running about yet, but he soon will be. We fixed his bronchitis and his other health issues, too. He's like a new pet, aren't you, my darling?'

But just as the corpulent professor went to pet Karl, Peter surprised us all by swinging round and punching him in the stomach. Swiftnick went down like a sack of turnips, sagging to the floor and making the waitress scream. Others around us noticed the kerfuffle. Someone called for security. Karl was barking by now, panicking as his lead yanked when the Dean fell on the floor.

'He hit me! He assaulted me!' Swiftnick wailed.

Peter didn't waste any time at all. He bundled Karl into his arms and whipped the chain out of his enemy's hand. Then he turned to me with a quick, 'Follow me! We're getting out of here!' and he plunged into the thick of the crowd, protecting Karl with both arms.

I had no choice but to follow. We caused a ruckus as we ran, thrusting aside butlers and matrons and the City's finest citizens. The noise grew intense around us but I could still hear Karl yapping madly in his rightful owner's embrace. And we ran blind into the crowd. I couldn't recall the direction of the entrance and neither, it turned out, could Peter. It felt like we were running in circles through the crowd and soon they were jeering us like they were watching some kind of sporting event.

Then Peter found a metal stairway leading upwards. 'Come on, we can get out of here…'

I wasn't sure about this, but I'd have followed him

anywhere and helped however I could. We both went thundering up this kind of gantry thing that ran along the walls of the Planetarium in a great looping curve. It rose quickly and soon we were pelting along a spiral taking us high above the heads of the partygoers. The chatter and the music were even louder here, as if the echoes were caught in the great bubble of the dome with nowhere to escape.

We kept on running, as cries came from below and folk noticed where we were, and Karl was struggling to be free from Peter's arms. Now we were level with the lowest of the glowing planets and they were even more impressive this close. You'd hardly have known they were models. They seemed like actual, genuine balls of flaming gas and rock wrapped in cool blue atmospheres. The beauty of them almost made me stop running and simply stare. But I couldn't let Peter down. We had to keep running. But where to? As we raced round and round the spiral, higher and higher, level with Venus and Jupiter and Earth and even the highest and largest of the imitation worlds, I couldn't think what Peter had in mind for escape – if anything. He just wanted to get Karl away from that man, and I couldn't blame him.

Right by Saturn and her hooped golden skirts we stopped to rest briefly, breathing raggedly. I hardly dared look down at the party below. The upturned faces were so tiny and featureless. They looked like dress-up dolls, like figurines with crudely carved faces. I started to feel a bit sick.

'There'll be a hatch at the top,' Peter said. 'Leading out onto the dome. And there'll be ladders. There must be, for when they send cleaners up to scrub the copper dome…'

'What?!' I didn't relish the thought of clambering up there, on the highest rooftop in the City, clinging on for dear life in my evening dress as the winter winds tried to rip us off and send us plummeting down into Ruskin District.

Karl was still yowling with discontent. 'What has he done to you?' Peter cried. 'Your legs … Lora, he's had Karl's own legs removed, and replaced with these awful metal things. He's … he's fixed him. Made him *correct*. That's what they want to do to everyone… And he's turned him against me, too. Karl doesn't recognise me anymore…'

At that moment we were interrupted by shouts from much lower down the walkways. About three loops down. 'Come down from there at once!' It was a very nicely spoken security guard, who let out three warning laser blasts with her hand weapon, just to let us know she was serious. The laser bolts ricocheted noisily, causing a few more screams from below. 'Give yourselves up, miscreants.'

'Miscreants!' Peter laughed. 'Just what we need! A thug with a blaster and a vocabulary!' Then he was up on his feet again, shielding Karl with the folds of his jacket, and hurrying in the direction of the very top of the dome.

I had no choice but to follow him right to the very end. I was his friend, and that's what friends do. Regardless of the danger.

The rest of the affair was a disaster, though. We didn't escape with Karl. How could we? The Planetarium had the best security available in the City Inside. All the City's great and the good were present. It was impossible to get away unscathed.

Sure, we found the hatchway Peter had known must lie at the end of the spiralling walkway. We had a few terrifyingly dizzy moments at the top of the dome, with the uncanny, impossible feeling of being suspended at the very apex of the galaxy and the distant party below. I held Karl – who had calmed a bit – in my arms as Peter wrestled the hatchway open and let in a vast, howling blast of midnight air.

I just thought: we will kill ourselves if we climb out there. We'll never make it down the sheer, frozen sides of that dome. We're going to be dead, and all for nothing. But Peter was in some crazy zone where he couldn't see sense or talk to me properly. He wouldn't take no for an answer. At last I was seeing his radical and outlaw side. The boy who had been shunned by society and who'd had to run away to live in the Den.

He took Karl back off me and started to clamber through the hole in the Planetarium's roof. 'Follow me?' he asked.

'Every time,' I assured him, as the wind whipped my fancy new hairdo to pieces and I was left looking wilder than ever before. Only a very tiny part of my more sane mind was telling me that I should just back down for safety's sake … and I could return to the ground the way we'd come…

But now I could hear more laser blasts and the thumping and clanking of guards climbing up after us. Their flashing bolts couldn't quite reach us, but were bouncing off the metal skin of the dome, and blasting into the glorious floating planets. There was going to be horrible damage to this amazing place, and I was sure we'd wind up getting the blame.

I took a huge breath and followed Peter out onto the surface of the dome.

Of course we fell straight into the arms of security guards waiting on the other side. They weren't fools, they had a rescue party just waiting for us, as soon as we clambered out of the hole.

Peter tried to struggle; he was just about out of control that night. Someone shot him. They fired off a blast and grazed his temple and scorched his hair. He fell like a rock onto the metal floor. Karl shot out of his arms and, with no great urgency, one of the other armoured guards snatched him up by the scruff of his neck.

It was hopeless. There was nothing we could do. All I

could see through the blizzardy snow and the whipping hair in my eyes was Peter lying there, crumpled up, and at first I was sure they had killed him. I dropped to my knees and tried to examine him. The scorch mark on his forehead was fierce and his eyes were closed but I could make out that he was breathing. So they hadn't simply executed him for running up a few gantries and going where he shouldn't. But he was in the hands of the Authorities now. And that was just where Peter didn't want to be.

It wasn't so bad for me. I got what amounted to a few nasty looks and a slap on the wrist. I was dragged back into the Planetarium and given a good scolding for interrupting the wonderful party.

They took Peter off somewhere and wouldn't tell me where. I begged them to let me take Karl for him, but they said the cat-dog belonged to Dean Swiftnick, who was there to greet us with a triumphant sneer at the bottom of the metal walkway. He cosseted Karl in his arms, kissing the little creature repeatedly. 'What did those nasty, rough children do to you?'

I was led away in shame. It felt like every pair of eyes of every gussied-up guest was looking at me. They were all tutting and acting shocked that I'd been the cause of such a noisy palaver.

Above our heads, almost all of the bogus worlds of our solar system had been ravaged by blaster fire. But whose fault was that? It wasn't down to us if those guards were no good at shooting. And the way they sent ricochets flashing all around, they could have killed a bunch of party guests, too. It was all a huge over-reaction.

But Grandma's reaction was even huger.

She couldn't believe a grandchild of hers could do something so wicked as to spoil what she called the party of the century.

Ditto Al and all the Graveleys. They all behaved like I'd murdered someone.

'I guess we won't be getting any more invites to fancy places,' was all Da said to me, much later that night, when they eventually let us go home. I was in disgrace. But at least I'd never have to wear a posh dress again.

That night I lay awake, full of worry about Peter. What would they do to him, when they realised he lived in the Den? We'd been foolish. We'd thrown away his freedom. And I didn't have a clue how to help him now.

8

I went about my duties feeling more woeful than Old Man Horace looked, and a whole lot dumber, too.

He was the man who could say hardly a word after what the Martian Ghosts had done to him, but he was still talking to me more than anyone in my family.

He passed notes along the workbench. In his own way he was trying to cheer me up.

'You're still the same Lora as when you was little, causing a ruckus like that. I'da liked to see their faces at that fancy party!'

He made it seem less serious somehow. He made it seem like the grown-ups were over-reacting. It said in *The City Insider* that the damage to the Planetarium itself would cost hundreds of credits to repair. Da read this out, adding that we were lucky no one had sent us a bill yet. I blurted out, 'But we weren't the ones firing blasters at the planets!'

Grandma simmered with fury for days. She wouldn't look at me straight or talk to me directly. It was starting to feel a little cramped and uncomfortable in that flat.

How could I have messed things up already? I should

have argued Peter out of getting so crazy. He did it all out of love for his pet, but it was obviously hopeless. I should have realised that and made him see sense.

I told some of this stuff to Old Man Horace. He was teaching me a few skills. With great patience and care he taught me how to hold the knife properly and to carve curls of soft wood into the shapes of beasts and men. He kept nodding and smiling, assuring me I was doing well.

'You don't give into them, Lora,' he wrote me at one stage, late in the afternoon on a day I was feeling particularly lonely. 'These City people have got it all wrong. They're in a dream and so satisfied with themselves. You keep on pushing. You keep asking your questions, girl. You keep your own mind, you hear?'

I read this and my heart grew lighter right away. I looked up to thank him, to ask him more about what he knew, but he was across the other end of the toy workshop. He'd carefully put away his tools and was winding his scarf about his neck and pulling on his coat. I called after him, but he didn't hear as he beetled off into the snowy night.

At least Old Man Horace believed in me, a bit, anyway.

Da didn't anymore. Well, not quite. He just looked perplexed and disappointed with me. He wanted to know why I couldn't be happier and settle in the City Inside.

'Because they're pulling the wool over everyone's eyes,' I told him.

'What do you mean?' he implored.

'All I know is, the folk who are in authority – they're all horrible. They're cruel and corrupt. The Graveleys. Swiftnick. There's not one of them you should trust.'

Da just shook his head at me.

Grandma was scandalised, but then, that was because Grandma was their new best friend.

Despite everything, as the days went on we kept getting messages from the Graveleys, culminating in an invitation to a fancy dinner at their place.

'Even her?' Grandma nodded at me, once her first wave of excitement had died down.

'Of course, even Lora,' laughed Da. 'And she'll behave, won't she? Won't you, Lora?'

'No more running about with security guards after you and everyone in the place spectating after you,' the old lady grumbled.

Al reappeared and checked that we'd be coming to this meal. It was important, he said, that our two families got along well. We were all going to be symbolically unified by his wedding to Tillian Graveley.

I pulled sick faces and tried to make him laugh, but he wouldn't. Even when it was just the two of us. I couldn't believe it. Al had changed into an almost completely different person.

While we were alone, I tried another tack. 'You've got

to find out about Peter. About where they're holding him, and when they're gonna let him go…'

Al snorted. 'Do you really think they'll let him go so easily? After the chaos he unleashed at the most prestigious event in the City's social calendar?'

I could have punched my brother just then, for trying to sound so superior. 'Snap out of it, Al! This is me you're talking to, remember? We gotta help Peter. We…'

'I don't have to help anyone,' he hissed ferociously. 'He's nothing to me. He's just some tramp you were knocking about with, teaching you bad ways and being a security risk. You're well rid of him, Lora. If you carry on talking about him and saying he should be set free, the Authorities aren't going to be too happy with you…'

It was no use. Al's will had crumbled and he'd given in. Promises of riches and a good, secure life with the Graveleys had lured him away. Well, maybe it was to be expected. He didn't want any more fear and uncertainty in his life. He'd just given in to safety and maybe I should too?

No. It was no good. I needed answers. Things were rotten here, underneath, and I knew it.

We were all dressed up again and taking another luxury vehicle across the City to dine with Al's future in-laws. Da was looking expectant and actually as if he was looking forward to the coming evening. When we were dropped off into the snowbound street in front of the immense tower block where the Graveleys lived I asked him how he could enjoy all of this. Couldn't he see that we were just being bullied around by these rich folks?

'Sssh, Lora, I've warned you to keep that stuff quiet,' he murmured. He nodded at Grandma, who looked livelier and more excited than she'd been for years. Al had bought her a new frock – all shimmery pink and gold. She even had a funny little tiara perched on her new hair. 'Don't say anything like that in your grandma's hearing,' Da told me. 'She'll report you. She'll tell them you're not playing along in the game.'

I stared at him. 'Playing along in the game? Is that what you're doing then, Da?' I admit my words came out more bitterly than I wanted them to, as we stood there in the cold, with our breath streaming out in long plumes.

'I'm doing what I have to do, Lora,' he told me. His voice was so low then, but it was dangerous, too, like he wanted to yell at me. 'Don't you think it makes me sick to drink and eat and talk to these people? Do you think I relish their company?'

'I just don't know…' I said.

'Listen, Lora. These people – these Graveleys and all the other high-ups in this City. They got knowledge, and they've got ways of finding out about things. We need to stay close to them. Because there are things we need to find out, aren't there?'

I could hardly stop myself from grinning and grabbing hold of him in a hug, right there in the street.

'These people,' he went on, squeezing my arm as he led the way into the building, 'they're gonna be able to help us. I'm sure they can find Ma and Hannah. I'm sure, with just a bit of playing along, we can get them to help us...'

Grandma must have thought we were whispering between ourselves too much then, because she came elbowing her way in. 'Edward? Will you take my arm?'

'Of course, Ma,' he beamed. He looked so handsome and more steady on his feet than he'd been in ages, leading the way through the gold and glass entranceway.

Al and I brought up the rear. We barely glanced at each other. It seemed so long since the last time I'd been here, when it was just Al and me in our flat in Stockpot.

Of course, the Graveleys were all very charming.

There were several other guests present. A blurry parade of distinguished types who spoke in high-pitched voices and squeezed each other's hands in greeting. Mrs Graveley was in one of her extravagant gowns, with layers of lace and all kinds of stuff heaped on top of her skinny, withered body. Just about all evening she had hold of Grandma's hand and she yanked her about the suite of rooms, showing her every luxurious item in the Graveley residence. She introduced her especially to every one of the other dinner guests. I heard Mrs Graveley use her own favourite word dozens of times that evening.

'She's just extraordinary… Her story, her life, the odyssey she has spent her whole life on … extraordinary … impossible and extraordinary… Have you met Mrs Robinson? She's most extraordinary… She's from Earth, you know … she was actually born on planet Earth and lived there… She has blue ice in her veins, rather than common old red Martian dirt … Can you believe it? She's extraordinary…'

And I suppose it was all true. My grandma was indeed a lady from planet Earth. And wasn't she revelling in the fact tonight? She simpered and preened and took their tributes with grace.

'Oh, well,' she protested. 'I was quite young when I left Earth. Still a child, really, when we embarked on our mission to the stars. We were all so young and brave, I suppose. I look back and think – was that really little old me? Was this little old feeble woman really such a heroic young girl, once upon a time?' Then she'd shake her head in wonderment at her own legendary past. I heard her repeat this speech, and variations of it, several times that evening. It got dizzier and more scrambled and harder to follow, the more champagne she drank.

Maybe she deserved all this. Being celebrated like this. We'd only got to thinking of her as a nuisance, after all. She was a crazy old lady, as far as her grandkids were concerned. No heroine or superstar.

Then the Servo-Furnishings came in, serving drinks

and little snacks and Grandma gave a shriek of delight. She cooed over the wooden robot who came round to serve aperitifs. His counterparts – the tall ticking clock and the hat-stand butler – were also occasions for real joy from old Mrs Robinson.

'Oh, you won't understand,' she said. 'But these are top-class Servo-Furnishings. I never thought I'd see the like again. We once had many, many of these beautiful, polished servants to help us in our lives. There were almost as many aboard our ships as there were human beings, but they wound down and failed or were broken up for spare parts when we crash-landed in the desert...'

The Servo with the drinks looked alarmed at her story. Broken up for spare parts? Crash-landings? These were all terrible things that made him tremble before her. All the delicate glasses in his cabinet tinkled.

'And all I was left with was one hopeless sunbed,' Grandma sighed. 'Can you believe it?'

How the others all laughed at this. We were ushered into the resplendent dining room and Grandma was still making fun of Toaster, and how her last remaining servant was utterly useless. 'Who needed a tan in the Martian desert, huh? We were all scalded to mahogany by the end of our first season on Mars. But there was I, lumbered with this terrible old robot...'

My ears were scarlet with shame and my blood was boiling angrily in my veins as I sat in my place, a long way down the table from the important folk. How could she talk like this about Toaster? He was the loyalist, the bravest, the most senior member of our family. Neither Al nor Da appeared to mind that the posh guests around us were laughing about him. I spooned up my thin, fragrant soup miserably, reflecting that it probably didn't matter anyway. We had lost Toaster anyhow, and none of us would ever see him again.

And then, as if things couldn't get any worse, the door flew open and in stepped one late-arriving guest. And he came bustling round to the seat next to me. He was the person I wanted to see least on the whole of Mars.

9

I had to spend the rest of that evening sitting next to Dean Swiftnick.

Everyone seemed to hold him in great esteem. It was like he was a famous person sitting amongst them all. I noticed the other guests taking sidelong glances at him and muttering to each other. The big fat old guy paid them no attention at all, as if he was used to being looked at like he was something special.

I did my best to ignore him, as course after course arrived at the table. I was just counting down the minutes until we could get out of there and home again. Even the delicious food wasn't enough of a distraction. My throat felt tight with tension and – I can admit it here – fear. I found myself kicking the legs of my chair impatiently as the night dragged on and just about everyone got up to make a speech, crawling up to the Graveleys.

Then Dean Swiftnick was on his feet.

'How splendid to welcome the Robinsons officially,' he mused. 'What an incredibly interesting and important family you are, my dears. And how wonderful that, through the persons of their youngest members, the

Graveleys and Robinsons are set to entwine their family trees…'

I felt like throwing up.

'And we are privileged to honour tonight Margaret Estelle Robinson – the Earth Woman!' He simpered tremblingly and raised a crystal glass and toasted Grandma. 'The only Earth Woman on Mars.'

Suddenly everyone was on their feet at this. 'The only Earth Woman on Mars.'

It was a funny way of putting it. It made me feel strange. Was it even true, though?

Grandma struggled to her feet to make a speech of her own, but she was too drunk by then. The Servo-Furnishings came bustling in to clear away our plates and to bring us dessert.

When we were eating sorbet with tiny golden spoons I asked Dean Swiftnick, 'Did you bring Karl with you tonight?'

He frowned, looking down at me as if from a very great height. 'Karl? Oh, you mean Emperor Karligula the First?' He smiled, very amused with himself. 'What a spoiled and demanding creature he is becoming! No, my dear Lora, I have left him behind tonight at Swiftnick Towers. He receives far too much attention and too many kisses and hugs when he goes about in public these days, and I fear his head will swell…'

Once dinner was finished, we milled about in the

swanky rooms and I was free to get away from the horrible old man. Before I could, though, he buttonholed Grandma and was soon buttering her up something rotten.

'What a beautiful complexion you have, my dear lady,' he oozed. 'Why I'd hardly believe you were old enough to be Lora's mother, let alone her grandmama! Why, you could be her slightly older sister, even!'

Grandma croaked with laughter and punched his arm. 'Get away with you, you rogue!'

It wasn't even true anyway. Grandma had a complexion like a woman who'd lived and worked on the Martian prairie for just about sixty years. She was leathery as a burden beast.

But Swiftnick had her attention now. 'My dear lady, I wonder if you would do me the honour of visiting me at my humble abode? Tomorrow afternoon, late, perhaps? I could give you the most splendid tea. I finish my work at the university early tomorrow and I would be delighted to play host to the Last Earth Woman on Mars…'

Grandma blushed and batted her eyelashes at him. 'Afternoon tea! How lovely! I'd love to do that. I hear you've got a very fancy Homestead in the north of the city?'

'Ah, nothing too elaborate. And much too large for just one bachelor such as myself. But I would be proud to give you the guided tour…'

'Then I should love to accept!' cried Grandma. Her eyes

were gleaming and her piled-up hair was coming free of its pins. She was looking really kinda drunk by now.

'Don't go,' I warned her. 'I know what he's wanting from you.'

Grandma howled with mirth. 'Lora, I'm an old lady! This handsome young gentleman surely isn't suggesting anything improper…!'

They both laughed at me, then, thoroughly enjoying themselves at my expense.

'All I want is to hear your stories,' Dean Swiftnick said. 'Madam, will you tell me a little about your life and times?'

Grandma beamed at him. 'Why yes, of course, my dear sir. I'd be happy to.'

I cursed inwardly, knowing that she ought to keep right away from him. But what could I do? Even Da could see no harm in it when Grandma gabbled about her plans for the following afternoon all the way home.

It was indeed a most impressive abode.

'My god, just look at that place!' sighed Grandma. She was half out of the window of our cab as it pulled into the driveway of the Swiftnick residence. The lizards' feet were noisy on the gravel, and it seemed to take ages to get down that long boulevard of bare trees.

'He must be worth a fortune, Lora, don't you think? I had no idea. And yet he's so personable and hardly grand at all, is he? He's such a friendly young man…'

Young man! I rolled my eyes. I remembered how he'd hovered over me, putting all the wires and stuff everywhere when he thought he was going to drain my brain in his laboratory. Well, he'd failed at that, so now he'd moved on to Grandma. She had a much longer and more valuable history than I did, of course. What would he do? Strap her into another memory machine? Hypnotise her and get her talking? Take her skull apart and simply remove her whole brain so he could keep it in his collection?

For all these reasons and more I had insisted on accompanying my grandma on her journey to the north of the City to take tea with Swiftnick.

There was a small party of Servo-Furnishings to greet us at the main entrance, and they helped Grandma down from the taxi. The lizards whickered with impatience, keen to return to the City, and Grandma clapped her hands with glee at the sight of those wooden robots.

'Really, Lora. It's wonderfully nostalgic for me, to be around devices such as these. I almost feel quite grand again!'

A tall standard lamp decorated in marvellously coloured glass led us into the building, and the other servants dispersed to go about their duties.

'Dean Swiftnick has asked for a fire to be lit in the drawing room,' said the glowing lamp in a high, flutey voice. 'He will join you both in a moment.'

Grandma luxuriated on a plush sofa in front of the fire.

'Oh, this is the life, isn't it? Can you imagine? How I was used to a life just like this, and then I had to live on that dirty old prairie, in the middle of nowhere. Just think about all that red dirt and the way we had to pick up sticks and move on all the time, every few years. The way we had to live, year after year!'

'I always loved our life,' I said. 'I loved the Homestead, and the desert, and…'

'Oh, hush now,' frowned Grandma. 'You just never knew any better, Lora Robinson. You were born a prairie child and there's no getting round it. Like your mother. You ain't never known better. You've no greater ambition than the burden beasts.'

I fumed at her, but just then Dean Swiftnick came hurrying into the room. I had to blink at what he was wearing. It was a long purple dressing gown, tied with a golden rope. And was that some kind of tassled nightcap he was wearing? He looked ridiculous. Like someone out of a Victorian electric book. And in his arms he was carrying Karl.

'Here's the Emperor Karligula, come to see you, Lora!' he grinned, and set Karl down on the plush carpet.

The little cat-dog seemed uncertain at first on his new cybernetic legs. He stood awkwardly, like he'd just been born. He yapped at the Dean, and then at us visitors. And then, all at once, he seemed to recognise me. He made halting steps over the carpet towards me.

'He's just too adorable,' laughed Grandma, shaking the Dean's hand. 'And he's got miniature versions of my own miraculous leg. Ha!' At this she rapped her knuckles on her metal thigh.

'Karl…?' I asked, as the small creature lolloped towards me.

Swiftnick gathered him back up in his arms. 'Now, can I hear the approach of the Hostess Trolley? Hm? Ladies, it's time for tea!'

The Hostess Trolley was steam-powered and had a robotic mind of its own, and so didn't need a maid to push it into the drawing room. Grandma made cooing noises of pleasure as the trolley wheeled its way in, tooting out little puffs of steam as its kettle boiled. The plates of delicately cut sandwiches and cakes did look a bit enticing, it must be said.

And I was hungry, so I stupidly ate too much as Dean Swiftnick chatted up Grandma. I ate egg and ham sandwiches, and some kind of rare, smoked fish. And then little butterfly cakes and a squashy slice of cream roll with jam.

Grandma was munching away, too. She barely paused for breath as she set about telling Swiftnick all her old-time stories. Well, I'd heard most of them before. I already knew about her brother Thomas and her friend Ruby and the adventures they'd had aboard the *Melville* as it swam through the inky skies between Earth and Mars. I'd already heard quite a lot about the triumphs and then the disasters of Grandma's space-faring generation.

But it was all brand new to Dean Swiftnick. He sat beside her on the overstuffed settee, all agog at her every word. Karl sat on his lap, and even the cat-dog appeared to be listening.

After perhaps as long as twenty minutes I realised that Dean Swiftnick hadn't touched a single morsel of food from the robot hostess trolley. Nor had he taken a single sip of tea.

I put down my cup. Yes, it did taste a bit peculiar. Bitter. I'd just assumed it was fancy tea, and was meant to taste like that. Just as the unfamiliar salad leaves in the triangular sandwiches had a slightly sour aftertaste, as well.

Oh, no.

I watched Grandma as she described the earliest dwellings and settlers in the very first Our Town, when she was only twelve years old. One moment she was in full flow, gabbing away. Then she went a bit spacey-looking and slid back on the settee. She toppled into the cushions. She was suddenly out cold.

'Grandma!' I shouted. Except, I didn't. I tried to move my jaw and get my words out, but I couldn't budge. I couldn't make a single noise. I felt myself slipping backwards into my own chair.

The last thing I saw was Dean Swiftnick grinning at Grandma's collapsed body and then sparing a glance at me as my eyes fluttered and my limbs stirred and I tried my hardest to fight against whatever had frozen me like this.

'Oh dear,' the Dean of the University sighed. 'A little tired, are we, ladies? Such an exciting time you've had of it, recently, haven't you? Well, it can't be helped. Margaret, that was such a scintillating oral history you were giving us about your past. Really very interesting indeed. Precisely all the information I need. But I don't suppose you'd mind if I had you carted off to my laboratory in the cellar, would you? Then I can just simply rip all the knowledge out of your head with my Remembering Machine, and I won't have to sit listening to you whiffling on for hours.'

He smiled and stood up, clutching Karl to his chest. He beckoned the luminous butler to pick up Grandma and to carry her away. She was light as a feather in the Servo's arms.

I was growing woozier by the second. I knew I would soon be unconscious and as helpless as Grandma. Was there nothing I could do to fight it? We had both stupidly and willingly walked straight into Swiftnick's clutches.

Then a loud, robotic voice from behind me said, 'What should I do with this girl, Master?'

'Hm?' asked Swiftnick irritably, as he prepared to follow Grandma down to the cellar. 'Oh, her. Lock her in the dungeon. I'll drain her brain later. She's of less importance than the old dame. Now come on, chop chop! We must get to work immediately before the poison wears off…!'

All at once I was being picked up by strong, metallic arms. They were concertinaed and shiny and … somehow familiar.

'Hurry now, you foolish robot!' cried Dean Swiftnick, and led the way from the drawing room.

In my last few seconds before passing out completely I saw what – or rather, who – was lifting me up in his arms and carrying me.

It was Toaster!

10

'Toaster?'

When I woke up with a thumping head my first thought was for our old Servo-Furnishing sunbed.

The room was so empty and featureless that I couldn't tell where I was. The strange knockout poison had made me confused, so for a moment I even thought I was back in our Homestead in the past. I thought that Toaster was on my mind because he was bustling about the house as usual, going about his chores, stamping and shunting around the place, with illuminated sparks glowing in his glass chest unit.

But, no. This wasn't the Homestead. This was a smooth-walled room, with bars on the glass door. When I sat up everything came rushing back to me. Travelling with Grandma to this grand, ridiculous house. The two of us wandering straight into the clutches of the worst enemy I had ever made in my life. And then…

Then, Toaster!

Bigger and shinier than ever before. He was looking finer than even after his first make-over when we arrived at the City Inside. Someone had been taking extremely good care of him. But that wasn't the biggest shock about seeing him again.

The biggest shock was that he was like a different person.

He was just so unemotional. He picked me up and carried me here. I could vaguely remember being too weak to struggle, and trying to reason with him as he carried me down to the cellar. It was as if Toaster had gone back to being simply the robotic sunbed he was meant to be.

I stood up queasily. The light was artificial and there was no clock in the room. There was nothing in the room but the hard bunk I'd been passed out on. I had no idea how much time had gone by. My breath was sour and nasty. I was dying for the loo.

Could I have been mistaken? Maybe it hadn't even been Toaster at all? But surely, I told myself, there was only one Toaster on the whole of Mars? It was definitely him. His strange, mechanical face had been without expression, but I still recognised it.

Dean Swiftnick had wiped his memory. Suddenly I could see what had happened. He had made Toaster revert to factory settings, even though that factory must have been a vast amount of time ago, and on a different world. Toaster was now his mindless slave.

I stood on tiptoes to see out of the barred pane of glass in the door. There wasn't much out there to see. Just more doors with bars and old-fashioned locks and, at the very end of the corridor, a staircase leading upwards. So, did

Dean Swiftnick have a whole jailhouse down here? What on earth was he up to?

I already knew the answer to that.

Experiments.

The academic had talked about his experiments. He was fascinated by the human memory and by mechanical memories, too. He talked as if the past was something physical he could actually grasp hold of. He could put those greedy, squat little fingers into your mind and claw the history and the secrets out of you.

And that was what he was doing to Grandma right now, somewhere in that laboratory of his, with Toaster as his accomplice, and we were his test subjects.

This was really dreadful. I felt like I'd badly miscalculated the danger we'd be placing ourselves in by coming here. And Da would be waiting at home, worried about the time getting later and later and still no sign of us. Would he believe we were being looked after, that we were safe and having a nice time?

I was an idiot. And, thinking about it now, I wondered whether Da could help much even if he guessed at what was happening. He was weakened. He couldn't walk for all that long, he was short of breath and he tried to hide the pain he was in most of the time. What could he really do in terms of breaking us out of here?

No. It was going to be down to me. And the first thing was getting me out of this cell.

I used the bucket in the corner and then, when I returned to the barred window, I got a surprise.

Karl was out there.

It was still so weird, seeing the little cat-dog tottering about on four legs. I'd been used to seeing him so helpless, wrapped in his hairy blanket, his limbs all twisted up. But now – with a sharp tink-tink-tink sound, he was coming down the metal corridor and sniffing the air. Tink-tink-tink. He didn't look as if he was used to walking about by himself yet. He was kind of hesitant and shaky, but there was no mistaking his determination. His tiny black eyes were gleaming and his nose probed the air searchingly.

'Karl! Karl, it's me!' I started yelling.

Could he hear me? The glass was thick and protected. I saw one ear go up quirkily. Yes, he must hear my voice. But could I even trust him? He was Dean Swiftnick's pet now, surely? The old man had probably brainwashed him as effectively as he had Toaster…

Tink-tink-tink.

'Karl?'

Yes, I think he saw me then. My wild, helpless face at the window. Was I imagining it, or did a cat-dog kind of frown cross his face?

Then he turned and sniffed along the floor. He sniffed at door after door along that hall. I saw him scratch and whine at one particular door, not that far from me.

Then, with a sudden jolt of energy, Karl whirled about

and went dashing back the way he had come. Sparks flew out of his new cybernetic joints and I cried after him at the top of my voice.

When I quietened down I heard another voice.

'Lora…?'

I froze instantly. It was a faint voice. I couldn't see where it was coming from. 'Who is that?'

'Lora! It's you, isn't it? He's got you as well!'

There was thumping from the door that Karl had been scratching and crying at. All at once I knew who it was.

'Peter?'

'I'm here! He's had me down here for days … ever since that stupid party. How come you're here? And where are we, anyway? Is this the City jail, or…?'

'It's Swiftnick's own house,' I shouted across. There, I could see a blurry shape in the window of Peter's cell. There he was! 'Somehow he's had you brought straight here. And he's up to bad stuff! He's got my grandma in his clutches and Toaster's here and…'

I was gabbling like crazy, and Peter tried to tell me I had to calm down. We had to work out what to do, and how to set ourselves free.

Tink-tink-tink.

Well, part of that plan was already sorted out for us.

Would you believe it?

Karl had been off on a mission of his own. He came marching back down the sterile corridor with something metallic in his mouth. His tiny jaws were clamped tightly around … what was it? I squinted to see, and as he trotted closer I could make out a rusted metal ring. It had ancient jagged keys attached to it. They were swinging enticingly.

'Karl! Karl, you're brilliant!' I yelled out. 'Look what he's got, Peter!'

'Amazing, Karl! Wonderful!' Peter's voice was jubilant. He was just about tearful at the sight of his beloved pet. 'I knew it, Karl! I knew you'd think of something…'

I watched – hardly believing it – as Karl jumped up on those new hind legs of his and poked his snout at the keyhole of Peter's cell door.

'No way…' I gasped.

'He'll do it!' Peter laughed. 'He so will!'

The cat-dog had more patience than was natural for an animal. He took each key in turn between his teeth and notched it into the lock. He turned it oh-so-carefully. It took two, three, four tries and then – all of a sudden – there was a rusty cracking noise and the antiquated lock dropped off.

Karl leapt backwards, barking with delight as the door flew open.

Peter came rushing out. He was just a blur of purple velvet. I realised he was wearing exactly the same outfit he had been wearing days ago at the Planetarium. Of course he was. But now he looked dishevelled and ragged, but that didn't matter for a second.

I watched with my eyes brimming full of tears as he grabbed Karl in both his arms and danced him up and down the length of that stark corridor. Maybe they were both making too much whooping noise and were barking and howling with too much delight – but who could stop them? They were ecstatic to be back together!

I couldn't make myself heard for ages as they danced around. Karl was licking Peter's face all over and wriggling his metal legs. I saw Peter pause and examine those dangling limbs. 'Oh, Karl – what's he done to you?' But Karl didn't pause for a second in his licking and slopping. It was like the creature had kept all this feeling brimming up inside for ages and now he could let it all go.

'Hey…!' I yelled, louder still. 'Can you guys spare a thought for me over here? I'm still locked up!'

Peter laughed and set Karl down. Wiping his face on his sleeve he came dashing over with the keys and soon he was flinging open my door. I fell into his arms and I was pretty glad to see him again, too. Though I stopped short of licking his face and stuff.

'You genius, Karl,' he grinned, picking up the little animal again. 'How did you figure out what to do? How did you do it?'

Karl just looked very pleased with himself.

'We'd better get out of here smartish,' I reminded Peter. 'We've made too much noise already. They'll find us…'

He looked grim all of a sudden. 'And you said this is

Swiftnick's house? We're not being held by the Authorities?'

I nodded. 'He's up to bad business, I just know it. And he's got my grandma.'

Hushing Karl in his arms, Peter led the way out of the corridor. 'I was unconscious when they brought me here. I have no memory, really, of the time since that party and us going up to the top of the dome…'

'It's been a few days since then, and you haven't missed a whole hell of a lot,' I told him.

'Look, I'm sorry for going crazy at the Planetarium, Lora. I put us both in danger. But it was this guy, you see. I had to try to get Karl out of there and away from that man.'

I understood only too well. But when I closed my eyes I could still see us, preparing to clamber onto that green metal dome in the snow, with the blizzard whipping all around us. If they hadn't arrested us, I felt sure that we would have been killed that night. And so I couldn't rely on Peter being level-headed when it came right down to it. He was too reckless.

I decided I was going to be the one leading the way out of Dean Swiftnick's mansion. I was taking charge of our escape.

But first we had to find Grandma.

She could be a pain in the ass and she didn't even know what side she was on, but there was no way I was leaving her there.

11

Swiftnick's place was a storehouse of treasure.

That's what we found out, looking for Grandma. Each room was opulent with all kinds of gee-gaws. Everything we saw was more luxurious even than the Graveley apartment.

Something Dean Swiftnick had that they didn't: proper relics of old Earth. Who knew how he came by them? It was impossible to imagine how much he must have paid for them, but we saw paintings and statues and all kinds of Earth-type things on display. There were maps and sea charts of the planet our ancestors had left behind. I paused and imagined how excited Al would be about seeing these. He had always loved anything about the seas and oceans of Earth. One room was filled with stuffed fish all sizes and kinds, mounted inside cases. In the very middle of the room, suspended above our heads, was something gigantic, casting a shadow that blotted us out: a shark, Peter said it was.

There were more rooms. Room after room. Whole rooms dedicated to fragile china, cups and saucers and dishes made of porcelain thin as eggshells. There were rooms lined with framed photographs of Earth cities, and when we peered the places looked impossible, and filled with huge numbers of tiny people.

And then came the most amazing room of all.

'Peter, we can't keep looking at everything,' I warned him. 'He'll know we're free, moving about. I wouldn't be surprised if he had hidden cameras, keeping an eye on us...'

Tink-tink-tink. Karl led the way impatiently to the next room. He prompted us with a few sharp yaps.

But Peter lingered in the room that housed the most amazing discovery yet and simply stared at the vehicle.

It was about twice the size of the old hovercart we had on the prairie, and it was more sophisticated. It was a covered wagon with windows all the way round the outside and the cab was enclosed in smooth, dark glass for the driver to see through. It was sleek and aerodynamic. It would have had to be, I thought, for sailing through outer space.

Along both sides of the wheeled craft was painted, in extravagant, scrolling letters of gold, 'The Celestial Omnibus Company'.

Peter whistled. 'I wonder how he got hold of this? This should be in a museum, for everyone in the City to see. The official word is that none of these survived intact. Swiftnick must be very rich indeed, and powerful...'

I asked Peter, 'So is this one of the original machines?'

'One of the early twentieth-century Omnibuses,' he nodded. He had read a lot about the origins of the City Inside at the City Library. He had scrapbooks and clippings and drawings of his own back at the Den. He loved all of this historical stuff. Now he could hardly believe he was in the same room as one of the mystical, historical engines that had brought his ancestors to Mars, all that time ago.

They weren't my ancestors. So I didn't feel the same connection. Still, it was pretty interesting, I guess.

Karl yapped again from the doorway. He was right. We were wasting time.

But Peter couldn't help himself. He reached out with one hand and touched the door of the Celestial Omnibus. He longed for it to open and to allow him aboard. But that didn't happen.

Instead, the alarms went off. There was a great, howling klaxon and flashing lights. Instant headache and panic.

'You've done it now!' I yelled at him. 'Come on!'

We dashed through further rooms, crammed with even more fascinating and intriguing things, including one more impressive vehicle, which had the sleek, silver shape of the shark we'd seen suspended from the ceiling. It was huge, with some kind of silver fins arranged above it. But we had no time to stop and examine anything.

We entered a narrower corridor and realised with a shock that the furniture was struggling awake, each wooden piece.

A tall cupboard, a hat stand, a cheval mirror. They were each turning around to stare at us, and attempting to block our way. The house was waking up at the sound of the alarms. The cupboard raised tough wooden arms and they clubbed at us as we squeezed past…

At last we came to a broad hallway with a curving staircase that I recognised. 'This is close to the main entrance…' I told Peter, who had Karl in his arms again, for safety's sake. 'I remember this.' Though now it seemed such a long time since I had arrived with Grandma. I wondered how much time had actually passed?

An ancient television set on long legs and castors came wheeling down the polished wooden floor towards us. Its picture was flickering and blue, and the voice that crackled out of it was obviously Swiftnick's. His grinning face filled the whole screen as it bore down on us. 'You clever things! You naughty children! Fancy escaping so easily from my dungeon! *Heeee heeee heee!*'

I didn't think twice. I lunged forward and put all my force into the shove I gave that TV set. It rolled backwards on its little wheels and smashed down on the waxy floor. It went off with a very satisfying bang. The glass shattered and a cloud of smoke went up, choking us both for a moment. But somehow the professor's nasty laughter lingered: '*Heee heee heeee…!*'

We dashed past the smashed TV and headed for the main entrance.

But standing right in front of the doors was the forbidding, boxy shape of an old friend who had set himself against us.

'Do not make me damage you,' Toaster warned us. 'My safety protocols have been altered. I can and will injure human beings in order to carry out my orders.'

'All right, all right Toaster,' I said, holding up my hands. 'We give up. You win.'

Peter looked at me, amazed. 'This is your friend, Toaster?'

I nodded grimly. 'Swiftnick has brainwashed him. He's erased the Toaster I knew.'

The sunbed chimed with mechanical laughter, as he seized the two of us with his clamp-like hands. 'I am much improved. I have never felt so liberated in all my life.'

We were led straight back to the basement. But it was a different part of the massive building this time, where Swiftnick's private laboratory was housed.

It was a huge room, with all kinds of mechanical apparatus lying about. All of it seemed vaguely medical. It was like Doc Eaves' surgery back in Our Town, but times a thousand. There were tubes and vats of strange-looking liquid bubbling away. There were banks of electric machines blinking and buzzing. It was also very like the place they had called the Elizabeth Gaskell Memorial Remembering Room at the university, and sure enough, right in the middle, there was a padded gurney and strapped to it was my grandma.

She looked tiny and withered up, as if all those wires trailing off her head had drained her of life force.

'Grandma!' I cried out, but there was no response. Her eyes were shut and there was a horrible pallor to her face.

Toaster prodded and pushed us so that we were standing a little apart from Grandma. There was no chance either Peter or I could spring forward to start ripping all those connections and rubber suckers off her.

'Where is he?' I demanded. 'Where's Swiftnick?'

He emerged grinning from behind a tall stack of whirring, clacking machines. He wore heavy protective goggles and rubber gauntlets.

'Oh, my goodness! The two of you have been so ingenious and so very badly behaved!'

'Leave my grandma alone,' I told him. 'She's never done anything to you. She came here because you asked her nicely, and she thought you liked her company.'

He shrugged. 'Her feelings, or indeed, my feelings, are irrelevant in this case. What we are talking about is history, and human history is bigger and more important than any one individual person.'

'This is how he used to talk at the university,' said Peter. 'It's like he has no warmth in him. No sympathy for any individual beings.'

'Oh, I haven't, have I?' Swiftnick jeered at him. 'And

what would you know, you foolish boy, eh? Tell me. What's the point getting all weepy and upset about people? About creatures, eh? Like the way you were about that silly cat-dog.'

Karl yapped at him for this.

'I know, my dear Karligula,' sighed Swiftnick. 'I'm just making a philosophical point.'

'I don't care about your philosophical point,' I told him. 'I just want you to let my grandma go free. You'll kill her.'

He pulled a face. 'She's quite resilient. And she's doing some remarkable work. Watch this.' He clicked his fingers and a glass panel lowered itself from the ceiling, right above Grandma's body. At first I thought it was like a guillotine and he was going to chop her in half like the travelling magician that once came to Our Town and set up a show. But the glass started glowing with pulsating colour and we saw that it was a giant screen.

Shapes were flickering into life, and noises.

I couldn't believe what it was showing. How was it possible? That screen was suddenly a window into the past. Into Grandma's past.

Images of what must have been her life on Earth went scrolling past at great speed. She was very young, and there were glimpses of the home that she must have lived in as a little girl. Family faces. Robots shuffling about. Metal-walled corridors. Some of the faces seemed familiar to me … I thought I saw Al, but it wasn't. He was older than Al.

And Toaster! There was Toaster, when his face was friendlier and his glass panels were all intact. And here – resplendent in the morning sun, upended like the old-fashioned rocket it was – the *Melville*. The ship that had brought those settlers to Mars.

All we had ever heard about was the wrecks mostly buried in the desert sand. No one I knew had ever seen one intact and undamaged. But just look at that!

'Yes, see! See!' gasped Dean Swiftnick. He was just as astonished as either Peter or me. 'See how the past is preserved! It's all there, in her mind's eye. Just waiting … like pressed meat in an old tin, or dried fruits in a jar of brandy. See how the old lady yields up her secrets to me!'

On the truckle bed there was a change in Grandma's expression. She was no longer serene. Her face was twisting in consternation. Worse, now she looked like she was in pain. Her limbs pulled at the straps that held her to the bench. 'Noooooo…' She started gasping for air and crying out. 'Nooooo…!'

The images were coming thicker and faster now. We saw more faces and people living a life of luxury aboard that magnificent ship. There were banquets and fancy processions. Here came the Captain, covered in braid and medals. There was a ball and Grandma stared at her own gorgeous reflection. And standing with her… surely that girl was Ruby? Ruby who I'd only ever known as a gruff old lady in a man's white suit, here she was in a T shirt and jeans, laughing with Grandma. Going anywhere they wanted to aboard the ship, even down into its engines, deep within its bowels. Ruby's da was Chief Engineer and he could do anything. He was teaching Ruby everything he knew. She was free to go anywhere and she took her best friend with her…

'Nooooo!' cried Grandma, her voice getting more desperate, rising to a howl.

'Stop this!' Peter shouted. 'You're pushing her mind too far.'

For a moment I had been hypnotised by the things we were seeing on the screen. But now I could see what it was costing. 'You're killing her…' I screamed at Swiftnick. 'Let her go!'

'No, never!' the Dean whispered feverishly. 'This is too valuable. This is first-hand experience. This is … this is magical. If she must die to bring us this knowledge, then she must!'

I knew I was going to have to take action. I was going to have to stop this at once.

But it was already too late.

There was a great explosion from the banks of machines as they overloaded. It was a hideous noise, and then a great pall of black, greasy smoke filled the room. Grandma was screaming – and the screen above us went suddenly dark.

12

'Don't just stand there, help me!' he shouted at us, and Peter and I were suddenly helping the old man and Toaster clear away the wreckage of wires and bits of equipment. Toaster gathered up the tiny form of my grandma in his arms and Swiftnick made him take her upstairs, to the comfortable lounge we had sat in when we first arrived.

'She's all right, she's okay...' panted the Dean, looking a bit scared as he checked her pulse and listened to her breathe.

I remember how I felt when Peter had rescued me from the Remembering Machine at the university. It was worse than feeling sick. For a few moments it even felt like my mind wasn't properly back inside my body. Grandma had been very deep inside her trance and reliving the distant past. It must feel so much worse for her.

'What happened?' Peter asked his old professor.

'I don't know. The machine encountered some kind of obstruction, I think...' The Dean shook his head and then raised one hand for silence. 'Ah, I think she's waking up.'

All at once Grandma was struggling to sit up. Her eyes

were full of panic and her breath came in gulps, like she was stranded in a sandstorm.

'Calm down, my dear lady, you must calm down...' urged Swiftnick.

Suddenly I was conscious that Grandma was lying there in some kind of surgical gown. She'd be horrified when she learned what Swiftnick was doing to her.

She lay back on the cushions and stared up at us like she couldn't recognise any of us at all.

'Grandma?' I asked.

She narrowed her eyes. 'W-who?'

She lifted her hands in front of her eyes. They were trembling. When she saw how clawed and wrinkled they were, she let out a stifled sob and started crying.

'She's still half inside her memories,' said Peter. 'She must think she's still that young girl. It's like she's aged sixty years in a few moments...'

I turned to Swiftnick. 'What you do is cruel. She trusted you. She even liked you...'

His face darkened as he scowled at me. 'It's necessary work, child. You wouldn't understand. How could you?'

'You almost burned her brain out! How could that be necessary?'

Grandma looked alarmed at this, and shrank back on the sofa, covering her face with her hands. Peter went to put his arms around her, and Karl got ready to jump up on her lap.

'You never explain anything,' I said to Swiftnick. 'You just grab and take. Perhaps if you asked people, they'd tell you the things you want to know.'

He shook his head blearily. 'No, no. The knowledge is buried. Too deep. Too far away. It can't be accessed by asking. It can't simply be told…'

'What knowledge? What do you need to know?'

'I … I can't tell you,' he muttered. 'You wouldn't be of any use. What are you? Just some child. There's nothing in your memory but useless, recent stuff. I've already established that.'

'Well, thanks,' I said.

Now Grandma was fixing Swiftnick with a determined gaze. Her eyes were blazing intently. She had that familiar crazy look about her. 'You were in my mind. You went searching through my memories for … for…' She became distracted, and lost her thread.

'There is a … hole in your memory,' he told her gently. 'Like a hole in a broken vase. Much has leaked out.'

'I could have told you that!' she laughed suddenly, shocking us all. 'If only you'd asked, I could have told you that right out! Like she said. Saved us all a lot of bother! Yes! Yes! So much that I knew once upon a time has just gone. Leaked out into the desert sand a long time ago. Yes! Not much left! Just useless stuff! Hahahaha! Tough luck!'

Dean Swiftnick didn't grow angry in the face of her mockery. He simply sagged down. He looked about as depressed as I had ever seen anyone get. All that swagger and showing off simply melted away and he looked all at once like a sad old man in a fancy professor's outfit. He took off his goggles and sighed deeply. 'If only you people could understand ... how important it is. How urgent. Our whole lives here ... the life of every man, woman, child and ghost in the City Inside and elsewhere on Mars ... we all depend on this work of mine.'

Peter and I exchanged a glance at this. Could he be insane? Was he just lying? We both knew in that moment that neither thing was quite true. As far as he was concerned he was telling us the exact truth. This was Dean Swiftnick making himself absolutely plain to us. We didn't quite follow it, but there were no masks now. He thought there was great danger coming and that he was the only person on Mars who could do anything to stop it.

The hostess trolley arrived with a jaunty toot, puffing steam into the air and bringing a fresh samovar of tea. Toaster went to pour us all a hot, sweet cup, serving Grandma first. She started to revive properly with her very first sip.

Professor Swiftnick was still mumbling to himself, as if he was talking plans through with no one but himself. It was like he was so clever he couldn't trust anyone else to share his burdens.

'You must tell us what's coming,' I said. 'And what it is you need to know in order to stop it.' My voice was very clear and very level. I didn't owe this old guy anything. He had done some awful things to me, my friends and my family. Yet somehow I had to understand what was going on with him. It seemed vital that I did.

'You can't help, you can't help,' he sighed. 'You're nothing. Just nothing. What good could you ever do?'

Before either Peter or I could reply to this, Grandma spat out her tea. 'Don't you ever say that to my granddaughter, do you hear?' She sounded more like her usual, sharp-tongued self by now. She looked just about ready to box Swiftnick's ears. 'She can do anything, our Lora. She's the best of all of us, do you know that? Do you understand?'

We all stared at Grandma and I just wanted to go over there and hug her. Just like I did when I was a really little kid, before she became too frightening, before she told me that 'big girls don't need to be hugging and slopping all the time'.

She stared back imperiously at us all. 'Well, thanks for the tea, dearie. And if that's everything you'll be wanting, I guess my granddaughter and I will be getting on our way. We'll be late getting home, I reckon. Come on, Lora. Help me find my things. We best get back. Your da will be combing the streets for us…'

The amazing thing was, Dean Swiftnick didn't try to stop us. It seemed that we weren't his prisoners anymore and he was happy to watch us wander out of his palatial home. He hardly said a word. Not even when Peter picked Karl up protectively, and the two of them marched out to the cab we'd called. Swiftnick didn't instruct one of his Servos to grab them and bring them back into his custody. It was like he just didn't care any more. His schemes had all collapsed and come to nothing.

Grandma settled into the back of the vehicle while I instructed the driver where to go.

'Goodness me! What time is it?' Grandma suddenly asked. 'What day is it? How long has that ghastly man had us trapped inside his castle?'

I couldn't even answer that. I dreaded to think what kind of a state Da would be in. Ripping out his hair in frustration and fear, I guess.

Swiftnick stood on the gravel drive, where the pink snow was turning at last to slush, and a warm sunlight trickled through the canopy of trees. Beside him stood Toaster, standing to attention.

'Toaster?' Grandma yelled out of the window. 'Are you coming with us or what?'

There was a pause as the old Servo looked from Swiftnick and back at Grandma and then shook his gleaming, reflective head. 'I am afraid not, ma'am,' he said. 'I belong with the Dean now. My place is here.'

'Ha! It is, is it?' she growled. 'Seventy-odd years mean nothing to you, do they? You'd rather have the run of a swanky joint like this, huh? Better than our pokey little apartment, I guess.'

'Indeed, ma'am,' intoned Toaster.

Then the driver cracked his whip, the lizards cried out, and our carriage went trundling off down the drive, back to the gates and the City beyond. It was such a relief to get away from that place and that strange, awful man.

'That Toaster always did have ideas above his station,' said Grandma sniffily.

I couldn't quite take it in. Toaster had been with us forever. He'd never let us down or even thought of betraying us. But it seemed like it was true. His mind had been tampered with so much he had become a completely different person.

'Grandma, are you all right?' I asked her, as the carriage was dragged through the streets of the City. 'You don't feel sick or anything?'

She pulled a rueful face. 'The sick thing is … why … inside, I feel like a girl of sixteen again. Those few ribbons of memory that man tried to drag out of my mind, they were pretty vivid. I feel like that same girl, even still, even now…' She shook her head in wonderment.

'At least he didn't get too far into your mind,' Peter said, stroking Karl between his ears. Karl wriggled with bliss. 'He's trying to say it was all for a good reason, but I don't trust him. He just wants secrets. At any cost. And I'm glad he never got yours.'

She laughed bitterly. 'He never got my secret history because it don't exist anymore. At least, not in my head. Not any more. I've forgotten more than that silly man will ever know…'

I guess that fact was true, and in the end it had protected Grandma and the rest of us, from whatever the professor had been planning.

Then, as the cab wheeled through busy traffic in the shopping streets of Bolingbroke District, quite close to home, she was struck by another thought. She leaned forward, looking alarmed.

'I did give away one secret I should have fought harder to keep…'

'What's that?' I asked, feeling hollow and frightened all of a sudden.

'Well, in those few bits of memory he got from me … if he looks back and studies them and thinks a little bit … he'll see that I am not the only living human being who was there back then. There is another one. One who knew more than me, even then. And one who is still running about on Mars to this very day. At least, she was until a few months ago…'

Was Grandma rambling? I couldn't quite follow her meaning. Who was she talking about? Had the machines affected her so badly that she couldn't make any sense at all? I looked at Peter, but he shrugged. He couldn't follow this either.

The carriage slid away from the pulsing, bright mainstream of traffic, through a narrow alleyway heaped with trash and days' old snow. Here were the tall, rickety fire escapes that zigzagged up all the buildings, and the dim, smoky lights of a thousand cheap apartments.

'Come on, Lora, think!' said Grandma. 'Who is as old as I am? Who knows even more than I ever did? And who's kept her marbles a bit better than I have?'

Slow, dawning realisation crept over me. 'Ruby!' I burst out. 'You're talking about Ruby!'

She nodded and grunted. 'Exactly. And if that Swiftnick is half as clever as he thinks he is, he'll be having her in mind as his next target. And he'll be deciding pretty quickly what he ought to do…'

13

It didn't take Professor Swiftnick very long to work out what Grandma realised in the cab we took home that day.

Old Ruby. She was to be his next target. Gruff, bluff, ancient old Ruby, whose Da was an engineer on the Earth Spaceships all those years ago. Ruby was the prize Dean Swiftnick – and the rest of the Authorities – were after now.

But how on Mars were they ever going to find her?

'They will need you to show them the way, Lora,' said a ghostly, sibilant voice at my ear. A very familiar voice. One I hadn't heard for several weeks. Since Christmas morning, in fact.

It was Sook. She came drifting out of the sky on her gorgeous brown and silver wings in the early hours of the morning. It was several days since our escape from Swiftnick's mansion. Several days during which we were amazed to be left alone.

Now, just as I was drifting into a light sleep, I was disturbed by a tapping at the window. I hurried over and shunted it open with my shoulder. It was freezing outside, but Sook wasn't even shivering. She was nervous, though, about stepping into the apartment. Of course. I'd only ever seen her in the open air. The Martian Ghosts would not be confined within solid walls.

I tugged on my jumper and went out to stand on the fire escape and she started talking at once. She seemed to know everything that had been happening to us already, and this puzzled me.

'Hold on, hold on, Sook,' I said blearily, waving my hands. 'Explain this to me. How do you know what went on? How do you know the Authorities need me?'

Her burning eyes revolved slowly. 'It's all they're talking about. Up and down their corridors. In their little offices. When you hover above the towers of the Authorities and peer into their windows, these are the words on their lips. They keep talking about the Expedition. They are taking the Expedition very seriously…'

'Expedition?'

'It is Dean Swiftnick's proposal, of course. He has the backing of the men and the women and the ghosts at the top. He will fund it himself. He is very rich, as you know. And he has the means, and even the equipment and the vehicle…'

'Slow down,' I urged her. 'An Expedition to where?'

'I can't slow down,' she told me. 'I must go soon. I wanted to come earlier, but they caught me and I couldn't escape for many hours, even days. They stoppered me up in a bottle, so I couldn't come to see you and warn you…'

In a bottle? Did she really say that? I looked at her wings and saw that they were crumpled. One of them even looked as if it was torn. 'What have they done to you?'

'It doesn't matter,' she said. 'I think perhaps they didn't want me warning you.'

'So they imprisoned you? And put you in … a jar?'

She nodded, pulling a face. 'It's the best way to disable us. In a jar with all this gluey stuff dragging us down and clogging our wings. Look, I've lost scales. It was murder flying here tonight. I can't get the height…'

I had a flash of horror at the thought of a creature like Sook losing her power of flight, and what that might mean for her. She'd be forced to walk about on the ground, the same as everyone else, and she'd stand out as so strange and alien. They'd treat her badly, I was sure. It was true, many people were strange in the City Inside, and not all of them were completely human. But none I had seen so far looked as non-human as Sook.

'Lora, they are coming for you and your family. The Expedition is on.'

'But where do they want us to go?'

She took a deep breath. 'Back into the wilderness. They want you to find your way back to where you came from. Before you came to the City. They want you to lead them to your Aunt Ruby…'

I gawped at her. 'But… But I don't know the way! How could I? I don't even know how far we have come… We last saw Ruby in those caves, with the lizard birds, and Ma and Hannah and the others … and it was you, Sook! You flew us away from that place. You brought us to the edges of the City Inside! Only you know the way, Sook! You're the only one who could find the way back.'

She looked alarmed. 'I can't … I can't go back there … I simply can't, Lora … They don't know and they couldn't make me, either. Please, you mustn't tell them…'

My mind was racing now. All I could think about was this Expedition. 'But … this is our chance! My chance!' I burst out. 'If they're looking for Aunt Ruby … well, then, if I help them, we can find Ma and Hannah! We all want the same thing! We can work together!' I was excited now, shouting at Sook on the fire escape and trying to make her see why this plan was a good one.

But she wriggled away. She looked stricken. 'I can't go back. I was burned. I got too close. If I go back to the wilderness I will be killed. I only came here to warn you, Lora. The Authorities want you. They need you. I came to warn you to get away before they seize you…'

'But, Sook, don't you see?' I couldn't understand why she didn't follow me. 'We can find my ma and the rest of our people. Not just Aunt Ruby. We can find Hannah. Even the Adamses and the dressmaker. They won't all be lost anymore! We could bring them here to safety, to the City…'

She stared into my eyes. 'I cannot help you, my dear.'

And she kissed me swiftly, let go of my hands, and stepped back off the fire escape. Sook streaked into the sky above the rickety rooftops of Bolingbroke District and she was as elegant as ever. But because I had seen her fly so many times, I could make out the wobble in her wings, and see that she had been damaged in her recent ordeal.

Why wouldn't she come back with me to the wilderness? Why wouldn't she help? I wished she would talk more plainly and let me know her reasons.

All I could think about was how Da would be amazed and delighted by the thought of me setting off to reunite our family. Could I do it? Of course I could. With or without the help of Sook.

'Are you out of your mind, Lora?'

This wasn't exactly the response I'd been anticipating from him.

Grandma poured us tea from the huge brown teapot that was her favourite and urged us to calm down. It came to something when Grandma was the calmest person in the room.

'You've only just escaped from that man's horrible castle, you and your grandma,' Da went on. 'Why would you willingly put yourself in danger again? You can't do this, Lora…'

It was frustration building up in him, that's what it was. For several days he'd been quieter than his usual self. Ever since our return from Swiftnick's place he had been pent up with fury. We'd been gone for more than a whole day. He thought we had been killed. The local police had simply laughed in his face when he claimed we had been kidnapped by a university professor.

'I won't have it, Lora. You can't return to the world outside.'

I was steadfast. 'I have to. It's about Ma and Hannah. You said it yourself, just recently. This is our chance to find them. We can use the Authorities to get them back...'

'Then I'm coming with you,' he said.

'Now, Edward,' Grandma interrupted. 'Don't be a fool. You know you ain't strong enough these days. Your leg was shattered. Your lungs are too damaged. How would you even breathe that hot desert air now?'

He opened his mouth to protest. Then he froze. His face was a picture of abject despair. He knew he was beaten.

'I am coming with you,' he said, determinedly. 'If there really is an Expedition happening, then I'm on it.' He added, in a quieter voice, 'But if there is an Expedition, how do you know, Lora? Who told you?'

'Just a friend,' I said. 'Someone who knows.'

'The girl doesn't know anything,' Grandma snapped. 'It's all in her head.'

More days passed and little was said.

I was almost tempted to believe Sook's late night visit had been a dream. In the gleaming daylight and dingy rain of the next few days it was easy to imagine that nothing had actually been said. There was no Expedition. There was nothing to fret about, no great ordeal that we had to face. Days went on with us trekking into the alleys and into the subterranean workshop, where we worked on creating those wooden effigies with Old Man Horace.

But then, at the end of the week, there was a great clanging and clattering on the fire escape.

'What the devil's all that racket?' cried Grandma, dashing out of the kitchen. 'Sounds like someone's dragging a hovercart up the stairs!'

Not long after there came a heavy thumping on the front door.

'Toaster!' she screeched, peeping through the letterbox. Grandma fiddled impatiently with the locks and flung open the door. 'You've had second thoughts! You came back to us after all! You came home!'

The flat face of the sunbed stared back expressionlessly at his one-time mistress. 'This is not my home.'

'But it is, Toaster,' said Grandma. 'Your home is with me and the rest of the Robinsons. You know that really. I don't believe anyone could ever mess with your head so much that you'd forget that!'

I was glad to hear that Grandma had changed her tune.

I knew that Toaster's defection had hurt her feelings. By now I was at her side and staring up at Toaster. He seemed taller and more menacing in the way he held himself.

'What is it you want, Toaster? Has Swiftnick sent you?'

'Yes,' he replied. 'He has asked that you all return to his home. It is time that we embarked on the Expedition.'

I played dumb. He didn't know what Sook had told me. He'd better explain things properly himself. 'What Expedition?'

Toaster didn't miss a beat. 'We know that you have received a visit from the Martian girl, Sook. We know the import of her warning to you. You must tell us where she is. She is important to us, too.'

'Martian girl?' Grandma frowned. 'What Martian girl? We don't know who you're talking about…'

Naturally I had never told Grandma about Sook. I wasn't about to tell her anything right now.

'I couldn't find her if I wanted to, Toaster. I wouldn't give her away, even if I could.'

He shrugged, and told us: 'You must accompany me.'

'Wait,' I said. 'What about Da? He's out just now. We can't just leave…'

'The male parent is of no use to this mission,' Toaster said. 'He is not joining the Expedition. However, both you and Mrs Margaret Robinson are required.'

'Me?' Grandma squawked. 'I ain't going on no Expedition into the wilderness at my age. Are you kiddin'?'

Toaster towered over her. 'You will all do as I command.'

'But must we go now?' I asked. 'Can't we wait until Da gets back, so we can tell him, and explain to him?'

'We must go now,' said Toaster, steadfastly. He raised his arm and grasped Grandma's skinny wrist firmly in his clamp. 'Aren't you glad to be going home?' he asked mockingly.

14

The Expedition. Trust Professor Swiftnick to make it sound so grand.

When I first met him, when I ventured into his office just before Christmas, I had found that his shelves were stuffed with accounts of great journeys and interstellar diaries from the waves of Earth colonists who came to live in the City Inside. Now, with this trip into what was to him the unknown wilderness of Mars, he was hoping to emulate the bravery of his forebears. He was hoping to be involved in something legendary.

There was nothing legendary about it as far as Grandma and I were concerned. This was our return to the prairie, nothing more.

When Toaster took us back to Swiftnick's mansion it was aboard a very smart machine that sat very high up on the road. The windows were thick and darkened so that no one outside could see us seated within. It was like we were watching the City streets on a screen as we went gliding by. Toaster sat in the driving seat, working the controls with skill and care.

I was startled when he drew the vehicle to a halt

although we were only halfway there. The hatchway lifted, letting in a blast of wintry air. Peter came hurrying aboard, clutching Karl in his familiar warm blanket.

'Peter! You're coming as well?' I was surprised. Grandma merely frowned suspiciously at the boy and his pet.

'I guess they think I can be useful,' Peter shrugged. 'I don't know why.'

I wanted to ask him all kinds of stuff – such as how Toaster knew where to stop to pick him up, for example, because the location of the Den was supposed to be a secret. And I wanted to ask him how Karl was getting on, but there was no chance to ask anything. There was just time to make a fuss of Karl, and tickle his belly for a while, as Toaster drove through an oncoming snowstorm and lectured us all about the amazing machine that Dean Swiftnick had been preparing for such a long time. It was a true marvel of the age, and we were all going to be so lucky to join him for its maiden flight.

'Ha!' squawked Grandma. 'Nothing's more impressive than the Spaceships I've been on. Nothing impresses me anymore.'

'This will, I'm sure,' said Toaster smoothly, casting a glance at her over his square shoulder.

'Well, bring it on,' said Peter.

About half an hour later we were back at Swiftnick Towers. I tried hard not to wish Da was with us.

One of the towers of that mansion wasn't really a tower at all. It looked like a tremendous onion dome, a smooth and beautifully curved building made of translucent green stone. It sat squarely in the middle of the huge dwelling and I hadn't really given it much thought, besides – wow, that's an impressive Homestead the professor lives in.

But, as we were about to learn, that green dome with the delicately pointed tip wasn't a part of the building at all. It was actually the vehicle that Swiftnick had been working on for years.

'Behold the Sky Saucer!' he exclaimed, ever so grandly.

Oh, he was loving all of this showing off. Now that he had our attention, and now he knew we had consented (had we?) to come with him, he was relishing his role in this drama. Now he was acting the crazy and brilliant scientist, togged out in a tweed suit and heavy goggles and a green helmet to match the Saucer itself. He also wore boots and clunky rubber gloves.

'Welcome, welcome, ladies, gentlemen, robotic beings and ambiguous creatures!' He shook all of our hands enthusiastically and even I had to admit he seemed a much more charming person when he wasn't engaged in trying to steal the contents of people's minds.

We all stared up at the polished underside of the vehicle. It was so perfectly curved and smooth I couldn't see how you were supposed to get inside. It hovered effortlessly in the courtyard at the heart of Swiftnick Towers.

But still we stared, duly impressed by this miracle of engineering. Even Grandma was silenced by the beauty of the machine. It must have been as large as our one-time Homestead, perhaps twice over. I wished Da could have been there with us, seeing this. He loved any kind of invention or sparkly, ingenious, brand new thing. But I knew at the same time we were right to come away without him. Had he been there, he'd have insisted on coming with us on this Expedition, and he just wasn't well enough.

'What do you think?' Swiftnick grinned at us. 'She's pretty fantastic, isn't she? My little hobby, you might say. I've been perfecting her for years. I was never sure I'd get permission to use her. The Authorities have been keen to get their hands on her … but she's just for me. She's mine … all mine!'

Grandma coughed impatiently. 'Have we had enough of the speeches? Can we get aboard, maybe? It's chilly for old bones out here.' Snow was settling in her curly white hair. It was settling on all of us, Karl was yapping in agreement. The only place snow wasn't settling was the sheer green skin of the Saucer itself. The vehicle gave off a gentle heat and a just-audible sizzle that melted all the snowflakes as they drifted near.

First of all, however, there was a farewell committee to face. Dean Swiftnick looked impatient that there were people encroaching on his moment of triumph, and his expression was downright surly as a whole procession came filing out of one of the doors that led into the courtyard. 'The great and the good have come to see us off,' he grumbled.

I stared in fascination at the strange crowd that gathered there. They were all dressed up in colourful and formal attire. There were guards in ceremonial robes, and a few grim-looking political types who were obviously very important. Mr Tollund Graveley was there, looking as smart and sinister as ever. He was accompanied by his daughter, who had brought a kind of mobile typewriter with her. It hung from a chain round her neck and floated in front of her. This was how she wrote stories for her father's newspaper on the spot, as they happened. She looked very serene and superior, tapping away like that.

However, I was more interested in the fact that my brother was with her. He had a camera, and his flashbulb was bursting with blazing light as he took pictures of us standing in the shadow of the Saucer.

This whole thing was surreal. I hadn't been expecting to see Al at all. I hurried over to him as soon as I got a chance. It wasn't the formal way of doing things, and Tillian Graveley pulled a face at my temerity, but she was always doing that. I hugged my brother hard. I hadn't seen him for what seemed like ages.

'Lora, don't make a fuss,' he said, trying to wriggle out of my grasp.

'I'm your sister and I'll hug you when I want,' I snapped at him. 'I hardly ever see you these days, now you've gone all hoity-toity.'

'Don't embarrass me in front of everyone.'

'Everyone?' I laughed. 'Who are they? Just the boring Graveleys again.' Al knew I didn't have much time for them. 'And who's that? On the stretcher?'

But it wasn't quite a stretcher. Now that I looked properly, I saw that the guards were carrying what they call in the old books a 'litter'. It was a kind of gauzy tent that they were carrying on long poles. There was a figure seated on cushions within.

'Who's that, then?' I whispered to my brother. Looking about the courtyard, everyone else had hushed up. They were all staring at this new apparition, each of them seemingly impressed.

'You're very lucky,' Al murmured. 'It isn't often that She comes out into the open air. The success of your mission is very important to Her.'

'But who is she?' I wanted to know.

Al wouldn't answer me. He just sank to his knees in tribute to whoever it was sitting in that litter. Others were doing the same. Only Grandma, Peter and I didn't copy them. Dean Swiftnick shuffled across the frozen cobbles on his knees towards the curtained litter when he saw one hand emerge from a gap in the cloth. It was a gnarled hand, with dark purple flesh and twiggy fingers that gestured at him to come closer. The university professor looked deeply honoured as he crawled on his hands and knees in the crimson slush.

We all tried to hear what the mysterious beckoning figure said to him, but the voice was way too whispery.

However, as their brief conversation finished I swore I could hear, from behind those golden curtains, a ripple of eerie laughter. '*Heeee heeeeee heeeee…*'

But then there was a fanfare played on tiny trumpets by the royal guard, and it was time for us to get aboard our experimental vehicle.

As Toaster and Swiftnick turned to the members of the Expedition I felt a hand clasp mine urgently. I turned to see Al and he was grabbing hold of me, looking worried. He was looking much more like his normal self. 'Tell me you'll be careful out there,' he said. 'Please, Lora. Don't do anything foolhardy…'

His words made me smile. I was glad. So he did care really. His true self wasn't actually lost forever. When I looked into my brother's wide, hazel eyes I could see that he was the same boy as ever, deep down.

For the first time it struck me what we were about to do.

We were going back to what the City people called a wilderness. But to us it was the desert. And it was the dead forests and salt lakes and wide-open prairies. It was home.

'Won't you come with us?' I asked Al. 'It's your home, too. She's your ma…'

He shook his head. 'They won't let me. I'm too much a part of their lives.' And the way he said it showed up a chink in his armour. I saw then that Al wasn't completely glad that the Graveleys told him exactly what to do all the time. There was still a part of him that could think for himself, and rebel.

Just then, without anyone else seeing, he reached into an inner pocket of his formal jacket. 'I've waited for the right moment to give you this,' he muttered. 'I managed to rescue it from our apartment in Stockpot Plaza before they threw out and incinerated all our stuff...'

He pressed the small object into my hand. I knew straight away what it was.

'Oh, well done, Al!' I grasped tight hold of the mobile phone that Da had bought him all those years ago. Decades ago, it seemed like. I stowed it in the pocket of my pinafore dress. Da had bought this device from the Adamses' Emporium in our town. Of course, it had never worked as a phone, and no one had ever expected it to. But it lit up and bleeped very satisfyingly, and it had taken tiny photographs of anything and everything Al had wished to preserve. I knew that in the memory of this miniature machine there were pictures of our previous life at the Homestead, and also a visual record of our journey into the desert. But more importantly, there were photographs in this machine that he knew might well prove very useful to our Expedition. And he didn't want the Graveleys or the Authorities or that strange woman sitting in the litter to know about them.

I kissed my brother goodbye.

'I promise to keep an eye out for Da,' he said. 'I'll explain to him how they made you go without him. How you had no choice.'

I nodded and smiled at Al. I felt a prickle of tears, setting out for home without my brother. He had surprised me today.

Now he was hugging Grandma, who was assuring him that of course she'd be all right on this adventure. It was just the kind of thing she needed to keep her spirits up; to keep her from falling into the doldrums of old age. And it was true: lately Grandma seemed more sprightly and excitable than she had for a very long time.

And then, all of a sudden, there were cheers as Professor Swiftnick touched a control on a remote device and a hatchway opened in the smooth underside of the Saucer. A golden shaft illuminated the cobbles below and a short staircase slid out to welcome us aboard.

'Fare thee all well,' cried out Tollund Graveley as we made towards this ramp. 'May you succeed on your Expedition. The hope of the people of the City Inside go with you all!'

So now they were being all friendly and reckoning they needed us, and were glad of us going off on this adventure.

But I still didn't trust any of them a single inch.

'Well!' said Peter, smiling broadly. 'Here we go!'

I could tell he was nervous. He had never stepped out of the City his entire life.

Me? I couldn't wait to get back to the wilderness.

15

Grandma was the only member of our Expedition who wasn't excited about lift-off or anything else to do with our flight.

'It's the first proper flight of the Sky Saucer!' cried Dean Swiftnick. 'My dear lady, how could you not be interested? I'm flabbergasted!'

She waved him away. 'Once you've seen one flying machine you've seen 'em all. This is just a plain old hovercart to me.' And she demanded to be shown to her quarters at once. She had a raging headache, what with all the noisy engines and her ears popping. Toaster led her away to the crew quarters. I followed to see that she was okay, and saw her settled into a rather plain room with a lumpy bunk.

Even as the whole ship tilted and swayed into the skies above the City Inside, Grandma lay herself down and went to sleep at once. Like Da always said, the old lady could sleep through absolutely anything.

When I returned to the bridge of this brand new ship I found the others were frozen to the spot. They were struck dumb with awe. We all stared out of the glowing window screens that filled almost the whole wall space of the ship.

The City Inside was a fine diorama all about us. It was like being in the Planetarium, but with glass buildings and steel structures rather than worlds. And they were moving and gliding so smoothly. Or rather, we were, as the Saucer slid through banks of low-hanging crimson cloud and slipped higher and higher into the upper reaches of the sky.

Look where we were! I used to think when I lived on Storey 202 of the building in Stockpot District I was high up. And when Sook held me by the arms and flew me through the dawn I thought that was as high as it was possible to get. But the Sky Saucer was rising, and it kept rising, and it kept rising higher.

Dean Swiftnick couldn't contain his glee.

'I knew I could do it! I knew I could make it! I shall be like the explorers of old…!'

It was like he was about to burst into song, seriously.

Peter looked a bit disgusted by him. He clutched Karl in his arms because the little cat-dog was distressed at the way the whole machine was rocking and jolting as it rose.

Toaster, meanwhile, returned to the control deck and seated himself smoothly before the array of glittering lights and switches. His clamp-like hands moved carefully across the dials and buttons and I wanted to ask him: 'Since when could you fly a ship like this? The Toaster we knew could polish shoes and dig graves and carry sheaves of corn into the barn. When did you change so much, Toaster?'

But I guess we'd all changed a lot in our different ways. We were all doing things we never would have expected.

'Do you recognise this part of the City?' I drew closer to Peter and Karl for solidarity. For comfort too, I suppose, so that I wouldn't feel so much like I'd fallen into the lap of our enemies.

'It's all moving so fast,' he said, looking queasy. 'Or rather, *we're* moving so fast…'

Even the floor beneath us was transparent and when we looked down it was into fleeting, flickering glimpses of the canyons of the City. They plunged down for many miles below us. The distances involved were almost meaningless and yet I suddenly felt sick with dread. I felt like the City was trying to drag us down. Its green glass steeples were stretching up to clutch and grab at us, to bring us crashing back.

'We're approaching the City's edge…' Dean Swiftnick told us.

In the blurring mass of buildings and the complexity of information streaming past the glass walls and ceiling it was possible to make out that things were changing. The buildings were smaller, more spaced out. They were older and shabbier, perhaps.

And then, all at once, it was like we had hit a wall. Not

a rock-hard wall made of anything like actual stone or metal. It was a wall of something like jelly, or hot, humid air. The whole Saucer juddered and shuddered and slowed like it had been caught in a net. Its mysterious engines whined and complained as it was forced to slow down. We all looked at Swiftnick for an explanation, but the noise was too fierce by then for us to hear what he was shouting.

I was convinced we were all about to die. We had trusted him not to kill us aboard this hideous contraption. Why had we been so foolish? Were we so keen to escape the boundaries of the City Inside?

Then, with a great screeching, howling roar of protest the Saucer seemed to leap in mid-air, forcing itself to make a vast effort at breaking free. The grinding of the engines was replaced momentarily with a hideous shriek of pain.

It was like we had ripped our way out of a living creature. Like the City Inside itself was a gigantic beast and we had burst through the impregnable walls of its belly.

The Saucer kept on flying.

Silence dropped over us suddenly and we watched as Toaster calmly altered our speed and our direction. The way he touched the controls reminded me of how he used to smooth the ruffled feathers of our hens, back on the Homestead, when they were rattled and scared by the storms.

The silence was oppressive, heavy. The screens all around us were blank. It was night-time in the wilderness. There was very little to see but a hazy purple gloom. Below us the ground was much the same.

'What was that?!' asked Peter.

'The City walls were rather tougher to get through than I was anticipating,' Swiftnick said. 'I knew they were an actual, physical thing, but I never quite reckoned on them retarding our flight. How very interesting.'

'There is damage to the Saucer,' Toaster informed his new master.

'They don't expect anyone to leave the City, ever, do they?' I said. 'It didn't want to let us go…'

The professor turned to look at me and there was a strange expression on his old, bearded face. 'We're free now, Lora. And we're out in the world. This is your world, more than anyone else's. We have to rely on you, from here on in.'

'Okay…' I said.

But looking at the indigo skies stretching everywhere around us, and with the green glass City somewhere far behind by now, I found I didn't have the faintest idea which direction we ought to take.

Luckily, Toaster had a few ideas of his own.

'The mountains,' he informed us. 'The caverns where we were captured by those avian reptiles. I believe I can find the way back there, at least…'

It was so dark and featureless, and we were all so exhausted by then, that Dean Swiftnick decided that we should all take the opportunity of grabbing some rest.

'Forty winks, eh? Good idea, hm? You'll find that there's a cabin for everyone. Even if dear Mrs Robinson has allotted herself the fanciest one. There's even a room for Toaster to recharge his batteries in, and to meditate away from the clamour of human beings…'

'Night all,' yawned Peter, accompanied by Karl, whose new legs clattered on the dark-green metal.

Before I went off to rest I wanted to ask the horrible professor a thing or two.

'Back at your Homestead … that person … whatever it was … being carried about, with those drapes around her … who was she?'

'Don't you know anything, Lora?' he asked, and his face twisted up with scorn. This was more like him. He'd been excited, almost friendly, during the time we'd been aboard his precious Saucer. Now he sounded more like the Swiftnick I had known.

'I don't really know anything at all about the City Inside, you're right,' I told him. 'It's a weird place. It's all secrets and hidden societies and people being shady. It's universities and authorities who want to bleed your mind dry and kidnap your grandma and wipe the brain of your family's sunbed. It's not somewhere I ever asked to go. I was taken there against my will, and so were other members of my family. To be quite honest, Dean Swiftnick, I think your precious City stinks to high heaven. And I'd be glad if I never had to go back.'

He chuckled at me as I ranted at him and when I'd finished he was laughing with delight. 'Oh, be careful what you wish for, young Lora! *Heeee heeeeee heeee…!*'

I took a step backwards. 'You're a Martian, aren't you? And Tollund Graveley, and his wife … they both laugh like you do, as well…'

'*Heeee heeee heeeeee!*'

'And the person you kneeled in front of … that was a Martian too, wasn't it? All the Authorities … you're all ruling over the human beings in the City, on all of Mars … you've got control of us all, haven't you?'

'Oh, Lora … you understand so little. You hardly know anything…'

'I know more about Martian Ghosts than you'd think,' I told him. I could feel myself giving too much away, but I couldn't stop. 'I know you want to eat us…'

'Eat you?!' He looked genuinely shocked. 'Eat you?! My dear girl, where on Mars do you get your ridiculous ideas from? Why would anyone go to all the trouble we have if all we wanted to do was eat you? Don't you think we can't find more delicious things than boring old human beings to eat?'

I shot back at him: 'So, you aren't human, then? You're admitting that?'

140

'I'm not entirely human, no,' he agreed. 'But isn't variety the spicy life? Is that the correct human phrase?'

'You're crazy,' I told him. 'And I don't trust you an inch. And I think we should never have got aboard this Saucer of yours.'

He shrugged and smiled and lit up his pipe. 'Well, that can't be helped. We've taken off into the vast scarlet yonder. We're off on our Expedition now, Lora, and if you've got qualms … well, that simply can't be helped! You can like it or lump it, but we're all on the same quest now.'

I thought I'd never be able to sleep.

How could I? This was terrifying. We were hurtling through the skies above our world. I don't know how fast. It felt like it must have been three times faster than the carriages that run through the Pipelines beneath the City. I couldn't believe my body didn't revolt against such an unnatural thing. Why weren't we all screaming and fighting for breath? How could Peter and Karl go to sleep?

Grandma didn't see anything strange in it at all, of course. I almost felt respect for her, the way none of this futuristic stuff disturbed her. I thought about how the Graveleys had dubbed her the 'Last Earth Woman on Mars' and I suppose they were right. She was something kind of special. Maybe I had underestimated her all this time.

I must have actually drifted off to sleep for a while,

because suddenly I opened my eyes and there she was, sitting at the end of my bed. Grandma was perched there like a leathery old lizard bird, blinking her wise old eyes at me. When I sat up suddenly she held out a cup of coffee. It was steaming and delicious.

'This is wonderful,' I said, inhaling the aroma. 'Thank you.'

At her best, this is what Grandma was like. She was concerned for our welfare. She fed us. She looked out for us. She wasn't always crazy.

'I never made it,' she chuckled. 'But I found the Saucer's resident Servo. She's a drinks and food dispenser. Barbra, she's called.'

'She makes terrific coffee,' I said, and blew the steam away and sipped contentedly.

'I heard you talking to Dean Swiftnick last night,' Grandma told me, lowering her voice. 'Really, Lora, you mustn't ask him things. You mustn't question him at all. That man has been good to us. Well, apart from the drugging incident, maybe. You shouldn't rock the boat … Also,' she added. 'You might not like the answers you get.'

16

When I stepped out of the Sky Saucer on to solid red rock my whole body felt grateful.

We had been flying for almost thirty hours and I didn't feel quite real. Sort of jumbled and quivering. Standing on the sandy ground came as a great shock, and it did for the others, too, who were wobbling as they stepped off the lowered ramp behind me. Even Toaster was taking a few moments to recalibrate his balance.

The Saucer had alighted on top of a massive plateau of scarlet rock, several hundred miles south of the City Inside. I didn't really listen to exactly how far Toaster said we had flown. Distances didn't really make sense when we'd been moving so fast. But it seemed that Toaster knew what he was talking about. He claimed that this jagged mesa contained the caverns and the tunnels where we'd once been placed in captivity by those intelligent lizard birds who sent us to the City Inside.

The mountains around us looked familiar, I had to admit. The deep gullies and canyons looked just like the ones we had spent those long, hard days traversing. Why, that seemed like a whole lifetime ago. Not just a year.

A hot wind whistled across the plateau as I watched the others examining our new surroundings. Dean Swiftnick was in consultation with Toaster by now, peering over the very edge of the giant rock. Peter, Karl and Grandma were standing together, clustered about the solid form of the new robot, Barbra. She was talking in a high, fussy voice, offering to make everyone some more coffee.

'It's too warm for coffee out here, Barbra,' said Grandma.

'I can serve cold drinks as well,' Barbra offered brightly, and her lit-up face squinched in concentration. There was a tinny thunking noise and Peter looked down, surprised by a slot in her metal body, somewhere near the ground. 'Cans of orange pop!' he laughed, and I heard the fizz of him opening one. 'Lora, come over! Hey, Barbra, you don't do cans of dog or cat food, do you?'

'Why, of course!' cried Barbra. 'I come prepared with comestibles for every possible occasion!'

The new robot was a bit bright and sparkly for my current mood, and even though I was thirsty, I drifted over to Swiftnick and Toaster.

Just how far were we from the City Inside? I was thinking back to how Sook had taken us all in her arms that night, somehow, when we escaped from this place. She had made us hold hands and run and leap into the hot open air. And then, while we all slept through the journey, she had flown us an impossible distance … I wished I could ask her about it. I always had so many questions for Sook. Whenever I saw her they melted right out of my head.

'Is this the same place?' I asked Toaster.

'It is,' he said, flatly. I still wasn't used to his reprogrammed personality. He was so sharp and precise now. 'The colony of super-intelligent avians lies deep within this very rock. Their monarch's throne room is the last known location of the rest of the humans from Our Town.' He added the last bit of information for Dean Swiftnick. I was only too aware that this was the last place we'd seen Ma and Hannah and the others.

'Then we look for a way in,' said the Dean. 'And if we can't find one we must use the Phonic Blaster…'

I never had time to ask what that was, because at that very moment there came a whole lot of yelling from Grandma and Peter and, weirdly, from Barbra the vending machine, too. Karl was yapping madly. We didn't stop to think about it. We went running over the rocky plateau towards the Saucer again and it only took a few steps for me to realise what the source of all the distress was.

Three revolting creatures had appeared from nowhere and had surrounded our friends while they had been busy quenching their thirst in the heat.

I had seen such creatures before.

So had Toaster. He had been attacked by the very same entities when we were last here. These globular, featureless beings had set upon him and had covered him with some very nasty, sticky, jelly-like stuff that we had spent hours cleaning out of his metal parts. Now, recognising them, Toaster set off, faster than I had ever seen him move. He seemed dead set on having his revenge.

The creatures roared when they saw him approaching at speed. Grandma and the others fell back in alarm, keen to get out of the way of the furious, speeding sunbed. There came a loud, deadly crackle of energy and a savage bolt of green lightning.

One of the jelly-like guards screamed piteously as it was electrocuted by Toaster. Its appendages went quite still and purple fumes came rushing out of its many bulbous eyes. Then, right before our eyes, the creature withered up and dried. In seconds it had become no more than the size of an ugly baby doll.

The other two jelly creatures drew back in alarm.

'Ha! I've had a weapons upgrade as well as everything else,' Toaster shouted at them. 'Take that, you wretches!'

'Toaster, do be careful,' worried Barbra. 'They might be exceedingly dangerous…'

Toaster ignored the vending machine, as if she were beneath him.

Dean Swiftnick came storming into the midst of the group and demanded of the new arrivals: 'Who are you people? Why have you forced my Servo-Furnishing to defend us?'

The jelly creatures quivered and I thought it was

hopeless. They wouldn't be able to make themselves understood by us. I pointed this out. 'They can't talk. They're just low-grade servants. They're deadly, but stupid.'

Grandma looked appalled. 'Toaster, you killed one of them! Since when did you have the ability to kill?'

'Since about a fortnight ago,' Toaster snarled. 'Dean Swiftnick thought it might be useful on our journey.'

'And I was right,' said the professor. 'Now these two surviving creatures are so scared they'll do just what we want, won't you?'

Soon enough we were inside one of the smooth-walled tunnels deep inside the plateau. The purple shine on the walls gave me the feeling of being in someone's interior organs, like going down tubes and intestines … Peter and Karl looked about with interest as we went deeper and deeper and the way became steeper, the smell got worse and the air got hotter.

'Is this where you were before, Lora?' Peter asked me, remembering the stories I'd told him of our adventures on the way to the City Inside.

'It's even worse than I remember it,' I said, feeling terrible that we'd been forced to leave the others here, in this hellish domain. But of course we'd had no choice, and even here seemed preferable to the faraway and unknown place we were being sent to.

Ma, Hannah … could they still be here? After all this time?

The lumpish, grumbling jelly beasts led us further and further into the slimy labyrinth. They seemed very put out that we had killed one of their kind, but what could they expect? Before leaving the open air, one of them had extruded a tentacle and tenderly picked up the hard, dark doll and tucked it close to its body. 'They must have feelings!' Grandma cried out, and Barbra shushed her respectfully.

After what seemed like days the tunnel levelled out some. The passageways widened into caverns and the veins of luminous crystal in the rock walls became larger, brighter. Soon we were in chambers I was beginning to recognise. We were on the way to that vast throne room. The one with all the stalactites in its ceiling. Except they were swaying, stirring, living stalactites. They were lizards hanging upside down and staring at us with black, jewel-like eyes. They had made hungry snickering noises that could be heard from several chambers away…

But nothing could be heard right now. These rooms of polished rock were utterly silent.

Toaster realised this first. 'I can detect nothing,' he told us. 'This is not as it was before.'

Barbra shuffled ahead of us humans, as if she were making herself brave in order to save our lives. Since when had the Saucer's drinks machine become an integral part of our quest? But it really seemed that she had, and I was glad of another friendly face on our side.

We entered the gigantic throne room very cautiously.

Yes, it looked very much as it had done previously. The same ornate furnishings and carvings adorned the walls. Precious jewels and metals had been fashioned into friezes and reliefs to display the whole history of the lizard bird species. At the far end of the chamber lay the golden nest where the queen had sat and regarded us with such a superior expression.

Now there was no life at all in this sacred chamber. The phosphorescent veins in the deep arches of the ceiling showed them to be completely empty.

We walked towards the abandoned throne and found that as we stepped there was a horrible crunching noise.

'What are we walking on?' said Peter, letting Karl down to have a sniff at the noisy debris.

'Eggs,' said Dean Swiftnick. 'They're all dead eggshells, look. Long dead. Useless...'

Grandma made several noises of disgust. We were walking on the remains of these amazing, intelligent creatures. Creatures who had seemed so terrifying when I was here months before. Now there was no longer anything to be scared of.

We found the queen still on her throne-nest. Her golden feathers had seemingly weighed her down and preserved her shattered body. She lay there limply, curled up in death, unable to tell us anything about what had happened here.

Even the great glowing globe that stood so impressively by her throne was dead. At first its absence passed me by, because its ravishing colours and luminosity had been dampened down to almost nothing. Much of its surface was cracked and great chunks of the surface of Mars had been taken away. Stolen, perhaps. The remains sat there flickering slightly, lit by a dullish glow.

Toaster surveyed this wreckage with more regret than he had spared the lizard birds. 'I was depending on this globe,' he admitted. 'Its properties and the information it contained were irreplaceable.'

Inside my pocket, my hand instinctively gripped Al's mobile phone tighter. Only I knew that its memory contained actual photos Al had taken of that globe when it was still whole. For some reason I didn't want to declare that fact just yet. Right now I didn't trust Toaster, or his new master.

'Well, is this it, then?' Barbra asked tactlessly. 'Just a few old broken eggs and a useless globe?' She sighed, glancing about. Her inner workings began to rumble hungrily. 'See what even the greatest civilisations come down to, eh?'

Dean Swiftnick turned on her angrily. 'I do not care for philosophy from a coffee machine. Be silent or I will deactivate you, Barbra.'

She shut up at once.

'This is a setback,' said the professor, glowering at the devastation around him. 'I had hoped we would glean valuable information here. Toaster, would you scan what remains of the globe?' He handed out further instructions. 'Peter and Margaret, would you mind plucking the queen?'

Peter looked horrified. 'What?'

Grandma nodded. 'He's right, of course. She don't need her feathers no more, does she? And they'd be extremely precious. They could come in very handy…'

Peter went with her very reluctantly to fulfil this grisly task.

My thoughts were filled with my ma and Hannah. If this was what became of the deadly lizard birds then what became of the humans who were here? Or had they already left? Had they managed to get out of this horrible place in time?

The two jelly guards had been quite subdued since we had entered the wrecked chamber. The larger one was still hugging its diminished companion to its chest, and the smaller was glaring all of its eyes in our direction. I thought: we'd better keep an eye on them, and not underestimate how deadly they can be.

'What happened here?' Swiftnick asked aloud. His voice echoed impressively into the rocky rafters above. 'Do you have any ideas, Lora?'

'Something very nasty and something very dangerous,' I said.

And I said it just as a yawning pit of blackness opened up in the air right before me. It was darker than night, deeper than the canyons outside. It was silent and horrible and it opened with no warning.

The larger of our guards gave a terrified screech as it saw what I was looking at.

Even as it set off to run as fast as its legless body could carry it, the jelly creature was lost.

The Shadow Beast slipped through the hot air and fell upon the guard, easy as anything. It didn't even get time to scream.

17

'We've met them before,' I told Dean Swiftnick and the others. 'It's a Shadow Beast.'

Everyone drew back in horror as the empty patch of darkness reared up to its full height. Though it had no features at all, it seemed to be watching us very carefully.

'I've read of such beings,' whispered Swiftnick. He sounded like he thought the thing was awe-inspiring. 'In the early accounts of British settlers. They talked about the creatures that walked in two dimensions, that were thin as a sheet of paper. Creatures that could swallow men whole in the blink of an eye…'

And then it came back to me. I had a flashback to us standing in the blazing heat of the desert, and the Shadow Beast appearing from nowhere, and swallowing my brother Al's pet lizard bird. It had disappeared in an instant and it had seemed like we were about to follow him. But what was the thing that saved our lives and scared the Shadow Beast away?

The creature facing us here in the ruined throne room was even larger and more terrifying than the one I'd met before. Even as the memory of how to defeat it came back to me, it looked as if it were casting about, carefully selecting its next victim from our gang.

'Noise!' I yelled out, as loud as I could. 'That's what we discovered last time! These monsters must come from some dimension where there's no sound at all, and any kind of noise messes with their brains!'

My words were echoing brilliantly under the vaulted ceilings of the throne room. They came bouncing back, louder than ever and – yes! – the Shadow Beast was recoiling and maybe even shrinking a little.

'Come on!' I yelled at the others, who seemed frozen in fear. 'Make as much noise as you can!'

Suddenly they all realised what I was on about. Next moment, they were creating the biggest racket they could manage. Even the last remaining jelly guard was crying out, and making the strangest hullaballoo you've ever heard, out of all of its several mouths. Grandma was caterwauling fit to burst, of course, and Karl was yapping with all his might. Toaster and Barbra were turning up their volume controls as high as they would go and broadcasting their most ear-shattering electronic noise.

At last it was too much for the Shadow Beast. For some moments it twisted and turned and tried to back out of the chamber. It zipped about the place looking for a window it could escape out of. We stepped up our noise and the thing became more desperate. There was something wrong. It couldn't escape. It couldn't slip back to the dimension it came from. Soon it had diminished to the size of a hovercart, then a door, then it was only the size of a dinner plate. It was like darkness concentrated and intensified into a horrible black hole that led nowhere at all. It lay on the eggshelly ground and we kept up our noise, staring warily as it shrank down to the size of a credit note.

Barbra was the bravest of us all. She reached inside her own workings and produced a flask of coffee. She tipped out the contents and the throne room filled with that wonderful fragrance. But Barbra wasn't concerned with the coffee. She was squashing the now-tiny Shadow Beast into the flask. Then she quickly twisted the lid back into place, sealing the creature inside. 'There!' she beamed at us.

'Do you really think you can trap a Beast of Shadows within a coffee flask?' Professor Swiftnick sneered at her.

Barbra shrugged and popped the flask back inside her glass body. 'The flask is lined with silver. I've trapped the Shadows inside a mirror.'

Even Swiftnick and Toaster had to admit that the coffee machine had been pretty clever. And, as Peter pointed out, who knew when a creature like that of our own might come in useful?

'Right,' said Barbra smartly, as if she was suddenly in charge of our Expedition. 'I've had quite enough of this horrible place, and my ears are ringing, too. Shall we return to the plateau to consider our next move?'

It was good to be back aboard the Saucer. Even though everything being made out of green glass was a bit weird, the place was starting to feel a little like home. When the ramp retracted and the heavy door sealed shut with a massive whomping noise, we all breathed out in relief.

Toaster was at the controls immediately, preparing us for take-off. He was as keen as anyone to get us away from that plateau.

We had left behind the last remaining jelly creature. It had looked all forlorn standing there, a short distance from our ship. It had lost its two companions today and now looked completely bereft.

'I wonder if I should destroy it?' Toaster mused. He was still smarting from his earlier run-ins with the creatures.

'No!' Peter gasped. 'You can't do that, Toaster. Especially if it really is the last of its kind on Mars… Haven't we seen enough death and destruction today?'

Our sunbed merely shrugged and went back to fiddling with the Saucer's control panels. I felt a twinge in my chest, listening to Toaster's words. I longed to have the Toaster of old returned to us – he was kronky, often malfunctioning and sort of dithery – but above all he was kind.

Now he was entering the information he had gleaned from the cracked globe of the lizard bird queen into the Saucer's memory banks. He informed us of what he was doing with a great sense of self-importance.

'Will that help us, though?' I wondered. 'Is that going to tell us where Ma and the others went to?'

'Not exactly,' frowned Swiftnick. 'But we may get a clearer sense of how the land lies in this part of the world.'

Again I clasped hold of Al's phone, knowing that it would contain better, more detailed information. But still I held on to it, not quite sure why.

The Saucer's take-off and flight were smoother this time, as if Toaster was becoming used to the controls. Once we were coasting high above the canyons Barbra swung into action and started going round with hot drinks and little packets of snacks. 'I've not felt so useful in years!' she kept twittering. 'Serving drinks! Looking after everyone! Fighting monsters...!'

Hours went by and I spent them with Peter and Karl, on some of the comfier seats behind the flight deck. We could hear Grandma and Swiftnick chattering away together, and it was apparent that Grandma was studying maps and charts with the Dean. He was trying to get her to remember where her people had come from, and where they had settled in the vast, featureless plains. But Grandma soon became confused, and then cross because she felt that the academic was pushing her, and getting impatient. 'All these maps look the same to me. They're rubbish, there's nothing on them!'

'Just think!' Swiftnick snarled. 'You must remember something. Anything!'

'There was nothing. We lived on the prairie! There was nothing to see or to tell the land by,' Grandma protested. 'We lived in the shifting sands. Every season the storms came and blew everything about. It wasn't a place you could make good maps about. It never stayed the same one year to the next...'

'Pshaw!' huffed the professor, finally giving up on her for the day. 'There must have been something. You couldn't have just lived literally in the middle of nowhere.'

'But we did, didn't we, Lora?' she appealed to me. 'Nothing stayed the same, did it? Even the buildings we put up lasted less than eight years before needing rebuilding. Absolutely everything blew away with the red desert sand...'

I had to agree. I had spent my first fifteen years in that restless land. In fact, it had been shocking to me to discover the City Inside, and to learn that some of those towers and buildings and landmarks had been there for almost a hundred years. I could scarcely imagine such permanence.

Swiftnick packed away his papers and charts. 'We will talk again, old woman,' he promised. It was obvious that he had lost patience with her. He was no longer being all smarmy and polite. 'We will talk each and every day until your memory starts to clarify and you give me something more substantial than the waffle and nonsense you have come up with so far.'

He stomped off to his room for some privacy, and Grandma was left looking downcast. She came to sit with us on the relaxing chairs and Barbra bustled over at once with a drink.

By nightfall the Sky Saucer had left the canyons and the rocky mountains far behind. We were skimming closer to the desert floor. It was beautiful, but there was very little to snag the attention. Just the impression of a vast wasteland extending for hundreds of miles in every direction.

Peter joined me at one of the shining portals to stare at the sands, which looked silver in the Earth light.

'And you really travelled through these wastes in an old hovercart?'

I nodded. It seemed a lifetime ago.

'And you were in charge of all the adults? They listened to you?'

'I didn't know what I was doing, really. Just following the distant radio signals we could sometimes pick up. We thought they were poetical and mysterious. We tuned in and tried to fathom where these human voices were coming from. Turned out they were traffic reports from the City Inside.'

'I'm glad they brought you to us,' said Peter. 'I knew, as soon as I saw you in those first news reports. You and Al and Toaster, when they were reporting on you wandering out of the desert. I knew you were important. I knew I was going to meet you. I was reading the papers in the City Library and I had this weird feeling…'

I smiled at him. Peter had certainly become pretty important to me. I was lucky to have met him, down in the market hall on the ground floor of our building. He spent most days there, playing his tunes on a miniature harp, just like the one Ma had played. With Karl sitting there at his feet. Why, Peter had even been playing the same tune as Ma, that first day I had met him. Ma's favourite Earth-type song, 'Show Me the Way to Go Home…'

Suddenly I had a horrible feeling of the creeps, all down my spine. I looked at Peter. It must have been a funny look.

'What is it?' he asked.

I hesitated. Maybe I was just being paranoid. Maybe I was spooked and too tired. I couldn't doubt Peter, could I? He had been my friend right from the first. He was always on my side. There was no question about it.

But wasn't it a bit convenient that he had just happened to be busking downstairs outside our very own apartment block? Playing that very particular tune on an instrument similar to the one my mother always played? Now I found myself wondering for the first time if he had been placed there in order to attract my attention. Was he being used against me? Or worse, was he part of some organisation working to draw me in? Was Peter part of the Authorities after all?

'Lora … you've gone a bit green…' he said gently. 'Are you speed-sick?'

I began to shake my head, but just then the whole Sky Saucer gave a savage lurch. Grandma screeched in protest and there came a clattering of pots and smashed china from the galley kitchen.

We heard Professor Swiftnick come hurtling out of his quarters and storm on to the control bridge. Toaster was fighting to regain control of the craft.

'What the devil is going on?' shouted Swiftnick.

Peter was tugging at my arm. He pointed to the desert floor below. All I could see at first was a horrible blur of silver sand and dark, scratchy vegetation. It all swirled into one as the Saucer continued to weave about.

Then I saw that the vegetation consisted of stark black trees, spaced out on the sand. They were whipping their branches about as if they could move of their own accord.

Peter cried out: 'I think … I think the trees are dragging us down…!'

They looked like dark fingers raking through the night air. They were clutching at us and I realised Peter was quite right. It was like they were trying to claw us right out of the sky.

18

'It's some kind of nightmare forest...' gasped Swiftnick. Now he was standing on the transparent floor of the Saucer. The wildly lashing trees seemed so much closer. We were lurching about, trying madly to cling on to the furniture, but even that was shaking loose as our ship struggled to break free.

'Toaster! Do something!' Grandma howled above the seething, gasping noise of the engines. 'Isn't this Saucer the most advanced ship there's ever been? Isn't it the strongest and the fastest?'

But all those qualities didn't seem to be doing any good at all. We were tilting at alarming angles in the invisible waves of magnetism the forest was blasting at us.

'How can the trees send out waves of anything?' Peter yelled at the professor. 'How can trees do anything like this?'

'We have no idea what the trees are like out here,' said the professor. 'Lora! What do you know about trees?'

I struggled desperately to hold on to the railing next to them, and quickly racked my brains. We hardly ever saw any trees in the prairie I knew. I dimly remembered living in a forest when I was very small. But they were friendly woods. They were the type that didn't go on the attack, and weren't interested in eating human flesh and drinking human blood.

But there wasn't time for me to say anything. The Saucer was getting the serious wobbles now, and there was a hideous rending noise coming from somewhere above us. Could any force really be so strong that it could tear solid metal and glass like a wet paper bag?

Barbra came tottering on her castors out of the galley and warned us all to cling on tight. We were going down. There was no way out of this. The Saucer would never break through. She could feel it in every fibre of her metal being: we were about to crash land.

Dean Swiftnick howled with misery. 'I have spent years building this beautiful Saucer! Decades, even! And it's only lasted two days!'

Grandma's laughter came echoing from under the sofa as all the lights went out. 'We told you that life on the prairie was tough! We told you it was hard to survive!'

And those were the last words any of us heard before the Saucer went down. There came a tremendous, grinding roar. It was like a million green glass bottles were smashed down on the ground, shattering all at once.

I was the first to regain my senses and I woke to a scene of horrible chaos.

The Saucer was ruptured, cracked in two. It looked like a vast green dish of lizard eggs, with all its ruined contents spilling on to the forest floor.

The black trees had drawn back, clearing a space for us. Their twiggy fingers were poised above the flames and churning smoke. They seemed satisfied at the wreckage they'd created.

I didn't have time to think about them, though. I was more concerned with searching through the bits of chairs and control panels and unrecognisable bits of debris. There were orange and green flames licking around the edges of the Saucer, and chances were the whole thing was going to explode at any moment. I had to find the others.

'Lora…! Lora, help me!' I recognised straight away the high-pitched warbling of Barbra. She was up on her feet and digging under a buckled metal wall, where Peter and Karl were both trapped. They were unhurt, though they both looked shocked.

The night air was freezing and black beyond the trees. For a moment it seemed even more dangerous, moving away from the Saucer. 'Peter, stay here with Karl,' I said. He had a nasty cut to his forehead, I could see now. 'I'm going back.'

I did it without thinking. I knew I couldn't let the others get burned up back there.

Toaster came striding out of the flaming wreckage. He was blackened and somewhat battered, but he looked heroic as he carried Grandma from the remains of the Saucer. She was unconscious, and looked so small in his arms. Her cybernetic leg had been loosened somewhere along the way.

'We're out, we're all safe,' I remember thinking.

And then it came to me. No, we weren't all out and safe, were we?

What about Professor Swiftnick? He was our captor. He was my enemy. He was the reason so many terrible things had happened to us recently. But I couldn't let him be killed in the wreckage of his ship, could I?

Well, maybe he was already dead. In those last seconds before we crashed he hadn't been clinging on to anything solid. Maybe he'd been dashed against the floor or the ceiling, all the life crushed out of him. Maybe it was hopeless even going to check.

Toaster placed Grandma ever so gently in the safe place with the others. She still wasn't conscious.

'Toaster, we have to save the professor,' I told him.

The old sunbed looked at me. It was a strange look he gave me. The lurid flames were reflected in his glass face and, for a split second, I thought I recognised a shard of his old, beloved personality. 'Why would you save him? Wouldn't you prefer to let him perish?'

But I wasn't going to argue ethics with a robot. I ran back to the Saucer, even as a fresh volley from exploding computer banks split the night air.

We found him beside his beloved controls. He looked pretty badly burned, but he was alive, and awake, and gibbering furious nonsense. 'Why does this always happen to me?' he shrieked with frustration. 'Every little plan! Every single, wonderful idea! Everything I pour my heart and soul into! All of it ends up in ruins! Get off me! Leave me alone! Don't try to save me!' He pulled away from us and sneered nastily. 'You human brat. You horrible girl. And you! You twisted heap of junk and misfiring circuitry! Don't shame me by saving my life! Don't even try! I want to die – here! In the ruins of my beautiful Sky Saucer!'

'He is hysterical,' said Toaster calmly, and touched Swiftnick's forehead with the metal clamp of his hand. There was a tiny fork of lightning and the professor passed out immediately. Toaster and I carried his portly body out of the mangled mess of his ship between us.

For about an hour after that, we all watched the Saucer burning. The flames seemed to keep the living trees at bay, and they didn't bother us.

'It won't explode now,' said Toaster, returning from damping down some of the worst of the fires with a phonic extinguisher.

We decided we would rest till morning exactly where we lay. The Servo-Furnishings would stay awake in case of further danger. The humans and Karl desperately needed to rest.

I remember Peter saying, as Barbra cleaned the gash on

his head with fizzy bottled water, 'Is it always this eventful, Lora? When you go on Expeditions?'

I told him that in my experience yes, they were always pretty hectic.

When it was daylight we woke up in ashes.

Some of them were green, from the Sky Saucer. Others were red but mostly they were silvery grey. The woodland around us was eerily beautiful. We stood up and walked around and the trees were quite still. Ominously still. We knew what they could do, though. We had seen them lashing their branches and dancing beneath us as they exerted all their might and dragged our sky ship down.

'Perhaps they can only move around at night?' Peter asked aloud. He was brave enough to go over to one of the gnarled trunks and press his hand to its cold bark. 'They really are metallic,' he said. 'Weird things.'

This was all ringing bells in my head. Memories were pushing at me. But where from? When?

Karl the cat-dog went lolloping through the trees after his master. There was so much joy in that little animal. It didn't matter what danger he was in. He was always full of happiness because he could move around by himself with those new legs of his. And he was back with Peter, after they had both thought themselves separated forever. I wandered after them through the dense, still forest, smiling at the way they behaved together. And I was wishing that one day I might have someone, or some creature at least, as devoted to me as that.

Right now I felt pretty lonely, I had to admit.

There was something very desolate about those woods.

But what was it? Why did I seem to remember them? I'd never been anywhere like this before, had I? We hadn't come this way on our journey from Our Town. The woods we lived in when I was very small looked nothing like this ghostly, horrible place...

Toaster and Barbra were calling me back to our improvised camp beside the wreckage of the Saucer. It seemed that Grandma was awake, furious and in pain from the near-removal of her fancy robotic leg.

Toaster administered a heavy painkilling sedative from a first aid kit I was sure he hadn't had before. It was tucked under one of his armpits, in a little cupboard, along with a needle attachment for his hand. Grandma stiffened and fell into a deep sleep, and she stopped muttering curses at once.

'I will carry her on my back,' Toaster said abruptly. 'When we move on from here. That is what you were wondering, wasn't it, Lora? You were worrying about how we were going to manage.'

I nodded. 'You're very clever, Toaster.'

'I was programmed in the first instance to protect the members of your family,' he said in his flat, dull tone.

'You're part of our family, Toaster,' I told him. 'You always were.'

'I am a simple serving mechanism,' he insisted. 'Any feelings I may have developed over the decades and any ability to think for myself have been expunged from my circuits by the professor. Those things were all aberrations.'

'No, Toaster, no!' I said. 'You were our Toaster. We loved you.'

'I don't need love,' he said.

I looked up, feeling awful. And then I felt Barbra's cold metal hand touch my arm. 'I'm sure he doesn't mean it,' she said. And just then the aroma of hot, strong coffee met my nose. Barbra held up a metal mug for me and I could have collapsed with gratitude into her concertinaed arms. 'Drink up,' she insisted. 'I'm sure I've got some fresh croissants, too. Or should have. I started baking just before all the ruckus went on last night…'

I laughed. Even in the middle of that awful forest and Grandma lying there with her leg hanging off, and us not knowing where to go next, Barbra the vending machine and hot coffee dispenser and bread-making oven on legs had managed to make me laugh.

'I'm glad you can find something to be amused at! I'm so glad to hear that you aren't overcome by misery and hopelessness!'

This was Swiftnick's voice. He was getting to his feet and looking absolutely livid. 'What have any of us got to laugh about?' he snivelled. 'We're all going to die out here. This is a wilderness. This is hell!'

I blew on my coffee to cool it down. 'Hey, don't thank us for saving your life, Professor.'

He stared at what was left of his Saucer. 'You should have let me die in there.'

'Someone's woken up in a good mood,' whispered Barbra. 'Have some coffee, Dean Swiftnick. It might perk you up.'

'Stuff your coffee!' he growled.

As I watched him stomp away I suddenly realised why I was in a better mood than perhaps I should have been, given the circumstances.

Dean Swiftnick was powerless. I had saved his life. I was no longer anyone's prisoner. None of us were prisoners anymore. We were free in the wilderness of Mars.

We might be lost in a forest populated by strange and deadly trees. But in a kind of way, I was home. We were all on my territory now.

And I guessed that meant I was in charge once more.

19

We pooled our resources. That seemed the most important and sensible thing to do right then. This involved checking how much food and drink we had. Barbra did a full inventory of her insides and told us she had fresh supplies of Krispy snacks and fizzy orange drinks and sugary biscuits. Grandma sneered at this, wondering how long such unhealthy, snacky stuff was gonna keep us alive in the desert. I had to point out that, without Barbra, we wouldn't have anything left to live on at all. Barbra looked pleased with herself. She did some calculations and announced that she would be able to keep us alive and fed for perhaps four whole days.

Four whole days! That sure brought things home to us. We had to find somewhere. Some destination. Somewhere with people. Somewhere fast. Otherwise we were going to be dead.

Dean Swiftnick's wounds from the crash landing were worse than we had at first thought. He had covered up the worst of his burns with his long, tattered coat. When he noticed this, Toaster produced all kinds of unguents and salves from his deep recesses. Swiftnick complained at being treated like an invalid, but he eventually gave in.

Then, when we felt we were ready, we set off.

We weren't really ready. No one had rested properly for ages, and most of us had injuries, scrapes or were coughing from the fumes of the Saucer crashing. But we knew we had to move on.

The woods creaked and the trees made strange whistling noises in the soft wind.

None of them were moving, at least.

But it was still daytime, and the trees extended as far as we could see. How far the forest went on for we didn't know. But we were sure we needed to be out of there by nightfall.

We kept walking through the ash and over the tangled metallic roots of trees. When, after an exhausting couple of hours, we took a rest, Barbra cheerfully poured us coffee and handed round some of her crisps. Nobody liked to say, but they were slightly stale.

Sitting there with the others, I made a decision. I had wanted to keep my brother's phone secret from them all. Well, from Swiftnick, actually. But needs must. I had access to information and it was unfair to keep it from them, especially if it might save our lives.

'What?' thundered Swiftnick, wincing with pain. 'You kept this … this … device secret?'

'Lora, how could you?' Grandma cried. 'I knew you were a selfish child, and a devious one at times, but to do this!'

'Calm down,' I told them all. 'It doesn't work as a

telephone. It never did.' I turned the small, boxy-shaped machine over in my hands. 'How could it work? Don't you remember how Al just loved it for the pretence of it? But also, for taking photographs?'

They all listened as I told them how Al had slipped me the device just before we had left Swiftnick Towers aboard the Saucer.

'Good old Al!' said Grandma giddily. 'He always was my favourite. Did I ever tell you he looks just like my brother, Thomas? And he's just as clever and brave!'

Peter looked concerned. 'But how do we know if the pictures on this machine are helpful?'

I shrugged. 'There's only one way to find out.' Turning to Toaster I clicked on the phone and waited to see how much juice it had left. 'It's almost dead … Toaster? Could you see what you can do with it? Can you extract the pictures we need?'

Toaster – although he was supposed to be back to his emotion-free factory settings – looked miffed that these pictures had been kept secret from him. He gently took the phone and spent some time connecting it to his circuitry. The rest of us just had to wait.

'Can we walk while you work?' I asked him. 'I'd like us to keep moving…'

Toaster answered in the affirmative. He brought up the rear as we went on slogging our way through the sandy and ashy ground, fighting our way here and there through tangled branches and fallen trunks. I glanced back now and then, and flashing images were spooling across Toaster's glass chest as he extracted the data we needed.

Then, at long last, we found we were coming to the edges of the forest. The trees were dwindling and the air was fresher, as if a new breeze was reaching into the metal woods and drawing us onwards. We were excited. We picked up our pace. We would all be glad to be free of these awful trees.

There was a horrible slope that was difficult to climb, and we really had to fight against the slippery sand to reach the top. It took twice as long as it should have, but when we got to the crest of the dune our reward was seeing that we had finally emerged from the woods.

And below us, for hundreds of miles in every direction, lay the desert. It was a soft, pale red. The sky was clear and almost the same colour. It all looked very beautiful. But it was pitiless and deadly. And it would obviously take us longer than four days to cross.

Toaster distracted us from uncomfortable thoughts like that.

'The images are ready for viewing,' he said. His metallic voice boomed out strangely in the arid air.

'More coffee? More snacks?' Barbra asked fussily, but no one wanted any more just yet.

We gathered round Toaster, shielding his glass panels from the glare of the sun. Then, slowly at first, but with increasing rapidity, he showed us the photographs from Al's phone's memory. First there were pictures of family – of Da and Ma and Hannah, and Toaster himself, and even the lizard bird Al had spent so long training and brought on our escape with us. There were shots of empty desert terrain as we began our journey, and then of the others who had joined us. The Adamses, Ruby … Al had taken many more pictures than I had even known about. He had documented everything we went through on the prairie with care, attention and even love. It made my heart twinge a bit with missing my brother.

But it was the very last batch of pictures that were the important ones. The images Al had managed to steal of the burning orange globe in the throne room of the lizard bird queen.

My brother had been very clever. He had got close enough. He had kept his hands steady enough, even with everything going on around him. He had taken nineteen, twenty, twenty-one pictures of the surface of that globe. Together they made a glowing kind of jigsaw and an accurate representation of this very part of Mars.

'Oh, my goodness…' said Swiftnick. 'That sneaky little boy. And you, Lora. These are treasures. These are priceless. And you had these pictures the whole time…'

'The question is,' said Peter. 'Can we use them? Will they lead us to safety?'

We wouldn't know the answer to that for a little while yet. Toaster was going to examine the charts and learn what he could from them.

At the end of that day we made a small encampment around a fire and tried to be as cheerful as we could. I tried to hide the fact that I was worried about what we were walking into. The heart of the desert would just swallow us up and we'd never get anywhere. Those were the thoughts pursuing me that night.

Barbara produced some eggs and a strange flat sort of griddle from out of her glass front, and she fried up egg sandwiches for everyone, which was a surprise and a treat.

Grandma sat there gloomily chewing hers. 'I just remembered something,' she told us all. 'About where we used to live. A landmark that a body would be able to see from the air even after all the desert storms had blown through.'

'Oh yes?' asked Professor Swiftnick. 'And what might that be, dear lady?'

'A lake,' she said. 'It was a mile from our last Homestead on the prairie. A dry lake. A cracked and parched lake that hadn't seen water in years. In centuries, even. It just popped into my head. Do you remember it, Lora?' Now Grandma was looking excited that her memory was coming back. It must have been all the physical exercise of slogging through the woods and then up the sand dunes. Blood had been pumping through her dried-up old brain and got it working again.

'It was a beautiful sight in the night, under the Earth light,' she sighed. 'Silver and blue like it was actual water instead of dust…'

Dean Swiftnick was frowning. 'So, if it shows up on the charts that Toaster is making from your grandson's photographs, then we will be able to find your home, your town … we'll be able to get our bearings in all this emptiness?'

Grandma nodded. 'I suppose that's true. We will.'

But where were Ma and Hannah, I thought. If they'd managed to get away from the lizard birds, where had they gone?

They were lost in the desert, weren't they? I knew all the answers already. They were lying dead somewhere in this hot sand.

Grandma wasn't thinking about the other members of our family. She was still going on about that silver lake.

I could see it all over again. The crazy zigzags in its dry surface. And that night … the night that the lake cracked open and all the shards of pale earth shattered into pieces…

'The night that Toaster threw Grandma's eyeball into the dead lake!' I said aloud, with a gasp. Then I realised that everyone was looking at me.

'What was that?' Grandma barked. 'My eye? What about my eye?'

Once upon a time Grandma had been the proud possessor of a false eye. An electronic eye from planet Earth. Something so futuristic and advanced that none of us knew half the miraculous things it could do. Grandma always said it ran off Blue Crystal Technology, and she could make it light up and shine like a torch beam, but even when we were little kids both Al and I knew that the eye was a kind of mystery even to Grandma herself.

On the night she had Disappeared and been taken from us, the eye had been left behind, accidentally. Toaster – Grandma's loyal and faithful servant then – had found it lying in the red dust of the road, right beside Grandma's cybernetic leg, which had also been tossed aside by her captors. At the time I had wondered if these electronic gadgets had been left behind because the Martian Ghosts had expected to find them less tasty and digestible than a fleshy old woman...

Now Grandma was studying me beadily with her only remaining eye. 'Are you saying you threw that precious organ away?'

'I did,' admitted Toaster, in his deep, rumbling voice. Did I imagine it, or was he sounding guilty?

'You threw away my eye?' Now she sounded peeved.

'We thought you were dead,' said Toaster. 'Inasmuch as I remember those long-ago events at all, your death was assumed by everyone. I deemed the casting of your eye into the lake of dust a fitting memorial.' He coughed mechanically. 'I believe I was a much more sentimental sunbed in those days.'

Grandma gobbled up the rest of her fried egg sandwich looking quite cross.

No way was I telling her the rest of the story. How her eye had flown in a huge, high arc through the night sky and, when it had touched down on the dry lake, it had set off an earthquake. How? Why? How on Mars was that possible? We didn't know back then, and we were none the wiser now.

Did we really want to go back to that strange lake?

And did I really want to go back home?

That night we all went to sleep early. It was cold and we had to huddle together for warmth. All except Grandma, who moved apart from us. She was still in a bad mood.

It was the night that Peter woke up in the very early hours. At first he didn't know what had disturbed him. Then he realised Karl had jumped up out of his arms. He had scampered away, to the top of the rise. When Peter caught up with him Karl was barking at something in the sand.

That was when I woke up, and followed after them to see what was going on.

Something was stirring. Moving gently. Something was emerging from the sand.

Something twiggy and sharp. First we saw one. Then

another, and then another.

'What are they, boy?' whispered Peter, looking ill at the sight of the things.

But he already knew.

They were bones. Finger bones. Hands and skinny arms.

They were skeletons coming up out of the desert...

20

My mind went back to the old stories. We used to tell them when we sat up late. In the Homestead, on nights like Hallows Eve. We'd be scared stupid of what might lie outside on the night prairie. This was the fault of Grandma and other oldsters. They would tell us stories about how poison vapours would come down from the skies and smother us if we left our windows open, or dared to step out of doors at night. They also told us the worst tales of all. The ones I found the most scary but the least believable.

I remember Grandma and Aunt Ruby scaring us silly over the very thought of the Bony Joes. They were skeletons who came climbing out of the sand. They loved to tell that tale, and I remember the Hallows Eve when Al was so scared he just about puked. And didn't the old ladies howl about that?

All this came seeping into my brain while Peter and me and Karl were stuck there on a ridge of crusty sand. Karl tried to bark and Peter stifled it, so he wouldn't draw attention to us. But how would those things we were looking at even hear us with no ears? If they turned round to look, surely they couldn't even see? They had no eyes, no mouths. They had no heads at all.

They were skeletons, just as the old ladies had described them. And they were rising headless out of the glittering sands. Hands first, clawing their way into the open air and it was like their pale, skinny selves were drinking in the Earth light. They loved it illuminating their joints. They stretched like they were sunbathing and the paleness felt delicious on their bones.

There were three of them standing there, stretching and clicking.

Then it was like they were looking for something, the three of them. They were hunting and pecking in the sand.

'They're looking for their heads,' I breathed. It was just like in the old stories. The dead bodies got up in the open air looking for something to adopt for new heads. And in the old Hallows stories it was pumpkin heads they found in the tangled vines. That's what I remember. But there was nothing like that here. Just the old skull of a Jack Rabbit, one from a lizard bird, and one we couldn't recognise. They looked very strange on top of the human-like bodies.

Once they had heads – even with empty eyes – they saw us and we had to run.

'Away from the camp,' I shouted at Peter. 'Lead them away from the others!'

It was a horrible pursuit, with the sand slipping away

under our feet when we tried to run faster. Were these shifting sands? I didn't even know if they were safe for running on. We could be sucked under, any moment. Maybe that's what the Bony Joes were leading us into? Maybe we were being drawn in and recruited?

Peter grasped my hand and we ran and we ran. The sands weren't getting us tonight. Neither were those horrible monsters. Karl started barking wildly, half-smothered inside Peter's jacket.

'What can we do? We can't outrun them.'

The skeletons showed no sign of slowing down. They wouldn't get tired. They would go on forever. They'd wear us into the ground and watch us sink. What would they do if they got their claws on us? I didn't even dare to imagine.

Peter was apologising, saying if he hadn't woken up, or gone with Karl to investigate the noises...

'I think they would have come after us anyway,' I panted. 'They would have found our camp and taken us from our beds.'

Just like the Martian Ghosts had done to the folk they made Disappear, I thought. But these were even worse, I thought, with their lack of heads and actual flesh...

We ran and ran, and every time I looked back those ghoulish things were still on our trail. They were messing with us. Waving and yowling with laughter. Letting us know we were theirs and they could catch us any time they liked.

When things were at their worst and I could see no way out at all: that's when I heard the voice I knew so well.

It was just inside my head. But it was like she was right there with me. I don't know now if she was there or not. But right then it was as if she'd swooped down from the sky just the way she used to.

Sook.

Sook's gentle voice. Right at my ear.

My flesh went prickling all over because it was like I could feel her breath on my skin.

She had good advice. She didn't waste any words with needless greetings or explanations. Sook just whispered to me: 'The feathers, Lora. Peter has the feathers from the dead lizard queen. They are inside his jacket. Throw them. Throw them away! And you will see…!'

She was gone all of a sudden. My guardian angel. But there was no time to think about where she'd gone to. I just turned to Peter and Karl and yelled about the feathers. They must've thought I was mad.

But Peter knew to trust me and he felt around inside his jacket and he produced a handful of those golden feathers. They were proper, tapered plumes. Very beautiful. Big as steak knives. Gleaming in the Earth light. 'What do we do with them?'

We turned and saw the skeletons were creeping closer. All playful, they were dancing towards us and waggling those mismatched heads. The empty eyes were so dark and horrible. There was a world of darkness inside those holes, far darker than the night itself.

Peter did as he was told and flung the feathers at the creatures. Kind of an elegant throw, like he was playing a game with arrows. And his aim was good. Feathers lodged in the bony ribcages and the raggedy jaws of our pursuers. Each of them burst at once into golden flames…

We both cried out. I don't know what we were expecting but not that. Not for the skeletons to become covered in a sheet of brilliant flame. They danced even faster, even more wildly. They lifted off their heads and threw them around the place, catching each other's and turning somersaults in the blazing air.

We backed away, Karl barking fit to wake the dead.

'Is it killing them? Are they dying?' asked Peter.

'I think they're dancing…' I gasped. 'I think they're enjoying it…'

But at the same time they were turning dark and crumbling to ashes as we watched. They dwindled and flickered and frittered away on the night breeze. And then soon nothing was left of them. The flames flickered and also faded away.

'Have you got any more of those feathers left?' I asked Peter.

'Just one,' he said, still looking shocked. 'How did you know they would do that?'

I didn't tell him. I didn't say much about Sook to anyone.

It was best that way, I thought. 'Let's go back and see the others are okay,' I said.

And they were. They were fine. But they were awake and frightened by all the hullaballoo. We both played down how frightening it was. How dangerous. How we had seen stories from Hallows Eve come to life that night. Where would telling the truth get us? Everyone was freaked out enough.

Too tired to sleep again, we decided to take advantage of the cool night by starting off on our journey while it was still dark.

Toaster led the way for us. 'The maps and charts aren't complete yet. I can't see the whole picture in my mind as yet. But I believe this to be the best direction,' he told us.

Soon there was coffee brewing and we set off once more.

Some of us were trying hard to forget about the Bony Joes we had seen and how they had hunted in the sand for new faces.

Those few supplies of Barbra's were something we were very careful with, doling them out day by day. Some meals we each had a handful, a small scoop of porridge or a few Krispies. With each meal the alarms were growing louder inside of me, warning that we must think again. I needed another plan. I needed to come up with something to help us along.

Mostly we kept calm. I think Barbra was a comforting presence, and so was Karl. Neither the vending machine nor the little cat-dog ever lost their spirits. They were always so happy and surprised by the things we saw on our long trek through the desert. Every little scrap of life or change in the landscape delighted them.

We humans had a harder time of it, of course. Grandma made things worse. She had become an ancient lady again. It was bad, but I was cursing her for her oldness and her infirmities. These were things she couldn't help. But the way she went on moaning and hissing and grumbling about every little thing – it was too hot, it was too cold, her legs were gonna drop off – it was almost too much to bear. Peter was good though. He would catch my eye and twinkle at me, or pull a funny face at the way she was carrying on. He offered to piggyback her, even though he was looking worn out himself by then.

Of course, Toaster was strong. He picked up Grandma like she was a half a side of pig or something. He slung her over his metal shoulders and she lay there helpless and relieved as he ploughed through the desert sand on his strong, square feet. I heard Grandma sobbing with relief: 'Oh, Toaster, you do care. You care after all. You remember! You really do remember the times when you were my only friend on all of Mars…'

Toaster didn't reply to her. The sunbed seemed troubled, as if memories were tumbling through his metal head. The images of the maps he was creating went flashing by on his glass panels and he kept his silence, trudging south.

That was where we were heading. South into the wilderness.

Dean Swiftnick was the only one of us who freaked out, oddly enough. He was the most educated and the most respectable, and everything. But it was he who just about lost his mind to frustration. It happened on the third day after that weird night with the Bony Joes, and we had spent most of an afternoon slogging up another tortuous brow of a hill. When we reached the top our vantage point revealed nothing but another sea of empty sand, stretching as far as the featureless horizon. Barbra busied herself brewing coffee and that was when the professor kind of lost his marbles.

'We've had it! We're toast! We're dead folk walking!' He gasped at the sight of us, calmly taking thimblefuls of precious coffee and sipping it. 'Just look at you! How can you keep calm? We're absolutely doomed...'

Toaster let Grandma down off his shoulders and she cast a caustic glance in the academic's direction. She said, snappishly, 'I thought you understood all about the perils of the wilderness? You always said you knew so much. You'd read all the accounts and the life stories of the British on Mars. Your precious Empire. Is maybe the reading about it not as difficult as the doing of it, eh?' Grandma was sneering at him. It was obvious she wished she'd never gotten us involved with this man and his crazy schemes.

'I didn't think it would be so … empty…' he told her. 'So meaningless.'

'Meaningless?' laughed Grandma. 'When you live in the wilderness you've gotta focus on surviving. There's no time for meaning. It's you folk in the City Inside, you're the ones worrying about "meaning" all the time. Busy as you always seem to be, you always got something useless like that on your minds.'

The Dean simply stared at her. 'Doesn't this emptiness around us scare you? Isn't it horrifying?'

Grandma just laughed. 'It takes a lot to scare a Settler from Earth.'

I was actually proud of my grandma right then. For the first time I could remember I actually felt like I loved her.

21

We trudged on through the desert.

I knew Barbra was almost clean out of supplies by then. I knew she was keeping that fact quiet. She was like a protective mother, hiding us from the truth.

Toaster was quieter than usual as the clouds settled down heavily into an angry purple mass right above us. The air was crackling with electricity like there was a storm about to begin. The tension in the air sparked off some kind of fault in Barbra's circuitry and she kept letting off bangs and flashes. She apologised every time, looking ashamed of herself.

Then Toaster cried out: 'I've done it! I've finished!'

We all turned to see what he was talking about. I think we'd kind of forgotten what he was working on. Now, in the gloom of twilight, he looked flushed with excitement. His face panel had a curious kind of glow.

'The maps?' Grandma asked.

'Indeed,' he said, and then started gabbling very quickly about how brilliant he'd been in piecing together the snaps my brother Al had taken of the glowing globe of the lizard queen. Grandma waved her hands impatiently.

'We don't want chapter and verse,' she growled. 'Just tell us where we are. And tell us what we need to know. Where is civilisation? Where is the nearest town?'

We were all excited now, even as the wind started to pick up. It whistled around the rocky promontory where we were standing, ruffling our clothes and hair as we gathered around Toaster.

'Give him his moment of triumph, Margaret,' Swiftnick said. 'Your Toaster's been working very hard. And he may just have saved our lives…'

'Well, Toaster?' Barbra said, encouragingly. 'What can you tell us?'

Toaster rose up to his fullest height and extended a silver telescopic arm towards the horizon. There the clouds looked an even darker, angrier purple. 'Two miles north-north-east.'

'Two miles?' gasped Peter. 'Is that all?' He looked excited. 'Then we've done it! We're saved!'

'Hold on,' I said. '*What's* two miles in that direction, Toaster? A town?'

Now the crackling charge in the air seemed to be getting to him, the same as Barbra. His face crackled and fizzed and disappeared for a second or two. '…At least there will … bzzz … be supplies,' he said. 'And shelter. And then we shall see. Bzzz. What we shall see … bzzzz.'

'He's on the fritz!' Grandma cried. 'Of all the times!' She forgot herself and jabbed him with her bony finger. There was a thunking noise and he buzzed miserably, trying to talk again.

'Come along, Toaster, I'll help you,' said Barbra, taking his arm and Grandma glowered at her.

'Come on everybody,' said Swiftnick. 'Two miles in that direction, he said. That's not far. We can do it. We know the way…'

But the air was getting thicker and darker and the wind came swirling about us. There was a gritty mist thick as sago pudding. It pushed at us, like it wanted to send us back where we came from. Keeping us away from where we wanted to be.

'It's a dust storm, I think,' I told the others. 'I was hoping it wasn't so. But it looks like a big one. Just like we used to get on the prairie…'

The others looked scared, all at once.

'Then we must hurry!' Swiftnick cried out, plunging forward into the gloom. 'Hurry! Hurry!'

But we didn't know what we were rushing into.

How far is two miles? How long does it take to struggle that far through a rising storm?

It seemed like half a lifetime.

Soon we were almost blind. The sand and grit were stinging our exposed skin. I didn't like to think about how the worst storms would pick the flesh off the bones of beasts left out of doors.

This was it, I kept thinking. This is how we'll all die.

This is where, one day, our skeletons will be found. Mars will make Bony Joes of all of us.

And then…

Oh, then, what did we see?

It seemed impossible. It seemed like it had materialised out of nowhere. It was like a phantom in the storm. A mirage from the sand.

A Starship.

One of the fabled ten.

Just its rear fins and the back end of its grand bulbous body could be seen sticking out of the sand. But it was taller than many of the buildings of the City Inside.

Our breath stopped. Our panic drained away. At the sight of the Starship, even the noise of the storm seemed to fade slightly.

'Is this what you saw on your map, Toaster?' shouted Swiftnick.

Toaster rallied a little. His face was still hazy with interference. He buzzed and squawked and then a few words leaked out. 'It's *The Emily Dickinson.* One of the ten iconic Spaceships from Earth.' His screen darkened and he didn't say anything else for a while.

Grandma was standing there with tears running down her cracked face.

'There's a breach in the hull,' Peter shouted. 'Look! Big as a house! We can get inside. We can shelter inside the Starship. The storm's getting worse…'

He was right.

But it felt creepy. Like we'd found a ghost ship and now we had nowhere else to go.

Whatever the great thick hull of *The Emily Dickinson* was made from, it shielded us from the worst of the storm. The crackling interference cleared from the glass faces of Toaster and Barbra. The howling of the desert winds reached us only faintly as we moved deeper into the ship, away from the breach in its side.

The two Servos shone their brightest lights hard as they could and gradually we could see more of our surroundings.

Grandma just stood there, staring.

Dean Swiftnick seemed to understand what was going through her mind. 'It's many years since you were aboard one of these,' he said quietly.

'The *Dickinson* was our sister ship. We were aboard the *Melville*, which was the most magnificent and grand. The *Dickinson* was basic and rather pokey…' She shivered. 'But look at it! Look at the things we created! Look at how we came to Mars.'

Now everything was calmer, Karl was eager to be set down on the metal floor. His replacement legs clicked and clattered as he stretched them. 'He's hungry,' said Peter.

'We all are,' said Grandma. 'Surely we can find something here, in the supplies or the hold…'

The hold – where was that? None of us had a clear idea of how the ships were arranged inside. I remember how those neighbours of ours, the Adamses back in Our Town, used to make regular forays into the desert. They had a bunch of Spaceships they used to search for fancy goods they could sell in their Emporium. It was stuff like tinned lobster and sugary bonbons. Everyone in town thought of them as grave robbers and thieves, but we were all keen to have a little try of what they plundered.

Peter and I wandered away from the others for a while. 'This whole place creeps me out,' said Peter. 'It's a tomb.'

'Imagine them moving through space,' I said. 'Ships like this. Swimming through the night, all the way from Earth.'

'I can't imagine what it was like,' he said. 'Was it noisy, do you think? Was it cold?'

'Grandma said they were kept in the greatest luxury during their year in spaceflight. All the furniture was alive, like Toaster is. Everything was alive and designed to help the humans on board.'

'Amazing,' said Peter. 'Your grandma belongs to a world we don't know anything about, really.'

We stood listening for a while to the distant echoes that filled up *The Emily Dickinson*. I remembered something about her book. It never seemed like no kind of story to me. All the lines had been pulled apart till they hardly made any sense. To be honest, I thought something had gone wrong with my electronic novel when I was reading Emily Dickinson.

One bit came back into my head as I stood there with Peter. One tiny bit of Emily Dickinson's book.

'The brain is wider than the sky.'

Peter looked at me. 'Huh?'

'I dunno. Just something I thought of. Something I remembered.'

'What does it mean?' Peter asked. He frowned. 'Maybe it should be "the brain is *wiser* than the sky".'

'Wiser? No,' I remembered exactly what I'd read. 'It was wider. Whatever that means.'

'I think I like it, though,' he said.

'Emily Dickinson wrote it,' I said. 'Who this ship is named after. I think she must have owned it maybe, or maybe she was the captain's daughter. Or she was the pilot. I don't know.'

There were more than echoes in the air. Both Peter and I heard something else. A low humming. Energy. Power.

Life?

We turned to look at each other.

Was there something in here with us? Was there something alive?

It was a thrilling thought. A frightening thought.

Then the noise from Grandma blotted it out. Grandma was shouting and screaming.

We'd wandered further than we had realised. Down

walkways and gloomy gantries, deep inside the ship. For a horrible moment I thought we'd never find our way back again, but Grandma was loud and getting louder.

Soon we could make out what she was yammering about.

'They're coming! They're coming here! For us! They've found us!'

'Who, Grandma, who?' I yelled.

Grandma, Toaster, Swiftnick and Barbra had all shuffled back to the hole in the flank of the ship.

No one had dug out anything to eat, but that didn't matter. The storm had abated some and the howling was dying down. But these weren't the most important things.

'Look! Lora, oh look!' Grandma cried. 'They've come for us!'

Through the swirling sand and dust we could see shapes moving on the horizon.

'Burden beasts,' I said.

'What?' asked Peter.

'Those are Prairie Folk,' Grandma grinned. 'We've been found!'

22

'Do you recognise any of these people, then?' Peter asked, keeping his voice down. He looked worried, I thought, and I didn't blame him.

They were togged up in their protective desert clothing: tattered furs and green leather jerkins and blue glass goggles. There were six of them. They had come thundering out of the last vestiges of the storm astride their burden beasts. To those who had never seen such a sight before, they looked formidable and fierce.

But to me they looked like Da and his cronies. They were like the men of Our Town who would ride about the prairie gathering supplies and keeping everybody safe. At the first sight of them I wanted to cry out in hope and longing. I hadn't realised until then how much I had missed my life from before.

'You came for us!' Grandma was greeting them, throwing out her arms as they dismounted.

Their leader undid the fastenings on his breathing mask and unwound the scarf from around his head. Soon his sun-cracked and whiskery face was peering at us suspiciously. To be more accurate, he was staring at the

Servos and Swiftnick suspiciously. They were the most unusual of our party. His desert eyes narrowed to slits as he tried to make sense of us.

'Who are you and where are you from?' he asked in his gruff voice.

Everything about these people was so familiar to me. I wanted to run and hug them. I wanted to clasp my arms around the necks of those green lizards they had arrived on.

Professor Swiftnick coughed to clear his throat and began talking in the pompous tones I hadn't heard him using for a while. 'We are visitors and explorers from the City Inside.'

'The what?' said the leader of the men, in plain disbelief. 'City of the what? There ain't no cities near here.' He looked round at the other men and laughed. 'You hear this? Cities!'

Swiftnick was blushing furiously. He was scared, sure, but his sense of superiority was rising up full strength again. He was gonna get himself into trouble with his attitude, I thought. 'There is indeed a magnificent city!' he said, his voice wobbling as if its very mention was making him homesick. 'Thousands of miles away. The City Inside is a wonderful place and from there we have ventured in order to...'

The leader of the men rolled his eyes and silenced the professor with a jab of his riding crop. He pointed to me. 'You. You tell us why you're here.'

It was because I looked like one of his own people. Parched skin. Broad, flat features. That was why he asked me. Grandma was old and loopy. The others looked soft and scared. The Servos were only machines. That was why the men turned to me. I asked them: 'Which town do you hail from, fellas?'

They chuckled at this. 'Which town? How many towns do you think there are round these parts, little girl?'

I could hear Toaster's circuits whirring. He was checking his newly minted charts. I just knew he was trying to come up with the correct answer. Not now, Toaster, I silently willed him. Don't go piping up with the answer now…

'I don't know,' I told them cheekily. 'But all we need is one town. We're dying of thirst and hunger. We been lost out here for days.' Oh my stars, I could hear the prairie accent surging back into my voice, thick as molasses. After months of keeping it down, making my voice more neutral so that the City dwellers could understand me.

Another of the men spoke up. 'What were you doing inside the Desert Ship?'

I looked at him. Is that what they called the Spaceships? Desert Ships? Did they even know where these vehicles had come from? What they had travelled through? I wondered if their town was even more backward than my own had been.

'Looking for supplies,' I told him. 'And sheltering when the storm came down. We were lucky.'

'You were indeed.' The leader of their pack studied us carefully. He appeared to come to a decision. 'I don't know about you lot. There's something strange about you. Something I don't trust.'

Barbra cracked at this point. 'Oh, please sirs! Please take us back to your City or your town, or whatever it is. You see, I have failed in my sworn duty to keep them fed and watered! I feel such shame! If you could help us and save their lives I should be so grateful, good sirs…'

'Shush, Barbra,' Grandma growled. 'That's enough. We don't need to beg off of this common rabble.' Grandma was going to get us all killed.

Luckily the men just laughed at her. 'Hold your horses, Granny,' said the senior man. 'There'll be no shooting. We're all on the same side. We're all human beings here, ain't we?'

We looked at each other. Yes, we were, weren't we? We were all human beings.

Professor Swiftnick looked abashed. He looked at the ground, as if he was scared of being found out, somehow. I remembered the way he laughed and the way he talked and once more I realised properly: the professor ain't fully human. He's a Martian hybrid. Of course he is…

'We're human and we're asking for your help,' said Peter and I had to smile. His voice sounded so posh out here in the desert, talking to men like those. They mimicked him and chuckled, but they listened.

They corralled us like beasts they'd found astray on the prairie and told us it was a two-hour journey back to their town.

'We can make it that far,' Grandma said, stiff with pride.

But I don't think we could have gone much further than that, as the sun went its highest and the temperature rose.

We set off.

We were going to a place they were calling 'Our Town'.

And yes, it was. It was Our Town.

Professor Swiftnick perked up from his drowsy stupor and stared at his new surroundings. His academic interest was piqued. His professorial eyes were taking in every last little detail. Peter was similar, in a way. He looked like he was being carried on the back of a burden beast into an incredible museum, showing him all these old ways of living. And when I looked through my companions' eyes I saw how primitive and rough all the wooden houses looked, and the red dirt roads running right through the place.

It was Our Town, but it wasn't Our Town. Not exactly. Not the precise one.

In another lifetime, months ago, I had visited a place we had called Dead Town and that was the spitting image of the town I came from too. It was like all these replicas were dotted across the prairies of Mars, and here was another one.

I was riding with the leader of the hunting pack that

had found us. I sat behind him on the leathery hide of the lizard and it was almost possible to believe I was back in the past, riding behind my da, the man was similar in so many ways. He was gruff and tough and short on words, just as Da had always been, back in those days. The smells were similar, too. The sun-baked skin and hide, and the smoky smell of cooking outdoors and the tang of engrained sweat and dirt.

Grandma rode into town like she owned the place, of course. She was like a queen in an old electronic novel, sailing down the river on a decorated barge. And the Servos were her slaves, marching alongside and gleaming in the heat. Only Barbra was limping along because her legs were seizing up and she clanked and moaned piteously, keen for a rest.

And here we were. In another half-strange, half-familiar town.

We were aware of eyes watching us from behind shuttered windows. The few folk out on the street were frozen where they stood, staring at us. Back in Our Town we might not have been the most welcoming of folk to strangers who came straggling in from the wilderness, but we surely didn't stand like this lot did. They looked struck dumb and helpless. Their mouths were hanging open. Their eyes were wide with … fear, was it? Why would they fear us? A girl, a boy, a crazy old lady, a useless professor and two kronky robots.

We had come out of the unknown, though. That was the thing. These people were used to their usual routines, the simple repetitive patterns of their lives.

'Look what we found!' the leader of the hunting party shouted. He jumped down from his lizard and the other men followed. They helped us – none too carefully – from our mounts and we were corralled in a huddle, in plain view of everyone.

'Look, we found strangers!' the man shouted again.

Figures started emerging from the wooden buildings. From the public bar, the storehouse, the town Emporium. Hesitant at first, the townsfolk came out and started gathering. They stared at us. We stared back. Grandma scoffed rudely. 'What are you lot looking at?' she jeered. 'What a scruffy rabble you are! What kind of lowdown dirty town is this, anyway?'

'Sssh, Grandma,' Peter told her. Karl was yapping on account of the tension hanging in the air.

'Don't you Grandma me!' she snapped. 'Look at this disappointing bunch! They look like half-wits! I thought we were coming to civilisation at last!'

Professor Swiftnick looked pained. 'Margaret, if you carry on like this they will refuse to feed and water us. They'll throw us back into the wilderness! Or even worse! Is that what you want?'

'He has a point, Grandma,' I said.

She carried on muttering to herself about what a

flea-bitten and filthy place this town was. How the folk ought to be ashamed of themselves.

'ASHAMED OF OURSELVES, EH?'

It was a huge, booming voice that rang out over our heads.

At the sound of it, everyone in the place fell silent. All the locals. All the hunting party. It was like they were used to that voice. They knew they had to obey it.

Our small party fell silent, too. Grandma looked furious. She was spoiling for a fight. But she wasn't in her right mind. She'd get us all killed.

'Who are you?' she cried. 'Come on out and show yourself!'

'YOU'LL SEE ME SOON ENOUGH!'

There was a crackle in the voice. I looked round and yes, it seemed to be coming out of the tannoy speakers that were fixed to poles at regular intervals down the main street.

And the more I thought about it, and listened, I realised that it was a woman's voice yelling at us.

'Who's that?' I asked the leader of the men.

'That's our Elder,' he said, pulling a mutinous face. His expression was dark, but there was no mistaking the fear in it. 'She Who Must Be Obeyed.'

'Show yourself!' Grandma bellowed. 'Come on, I want to see who we're dealing with here!'

My heart was sinking. All we wanted was some food

and water and rest. This was turning into another confrontation. Another frightening encounter on this journey of ours.

'VERY WELL,' boomed the voice from the speakers. 'I WILL GREET YOU IN PERSON.'

There was a moment of silence, then a clattering of wooden doors.

All heads turned in the direction of a nondescript building several blocks away.

A medium-height figure came swaggering out into the sunlight. She was wearing a white canvas suit and a broad-brimmed hat.

It took us a few moments of squinting at her before we realised.

Of course, Grandma recognised her first.

'RUBY!!' she screeched. 'What in the name of Jack Blazes and the Deadly Canals are you doing here?!'

'I am the Elder of these people,' Ruby called back, in a very dignified voice. 'And while in My Town you will all obey my every command!'

23

My head was spinning and it wouldn't slow down.

Ruby? Our Ruby? Ruby from Our Town, and Grandma's oldest friend?

She marched down that high street towards us like she owned the place, and by all accounts she did.

Grandma took a few steps forward and screeched out loud. Was it joy or was it fear? It was hard to tell.

A strange kind of change had come over Ruby. You could see at first glance she wasn't the same woman any more. She had hardened and set like mud in the desert. She had cracked and faded. She was rock hard and all her feelings were stored deep inside.

'What's the matter with you, girl?' Grandma shouted out. 'Ain't you glad to see us? Why, we dragged ourselves through hell to see you again! And me with one leg!'

Professor Swiftnick was coming back to life. He was quivering with excitement. 'This is she? Is this really she?' he warbled, pressing his hands together and staring at Ruby like she was someone magnificent, stepping out of history. 'The other surviving Earth Girl? Is that right?'

Everyone ignored him. We all fixed our eyes on Ruby as she stepped towards us. Grandma jolted forward.

'Keep back,' her old friend snarled. 'If the men think you're about to threaten me, they'll run you through and you'll be dead, Margaret. Just stand there nice and quiet.'

'Hurt you?' said Grandma. 'Why would I ever hurt you?'

'I have enemies all over this place,' said Ruby. 'That's the price of being the powerfullest woman in these parts.'

Then she stopped still and surveyed us coolly. She fixed her eyes on me in particular.

'Lora Robinson,' she whistled. 'Well, don't you look grown up now. You must of did all that growin' when you took us out into the wilderness with nowhere to go. Being in charge must have matured you and made you a woman.'

'I guess it did,' I said, trying to sound brave. But all the while I was aware that we were at her mercy. All I could think was: Ruby has gone crazy. The heat has driven her wits away.

'You left us there,' she said, with that snarl back in her voice. 'Inside that rock with those hideous lizard birds. You and your brother and that Servo. You left us to rot…'

'It wasn't like that!' I burst out. 'I had no choice! They forced me to go…'

And then – like dawn light coming over the edge of the prairie – a brilliant thought came into my head. That's how exhausted I was. That's how confused I was. I hadn't thought that thought yet. And now here it was. I burst out with it.

'Ma and Hannah…' I gasped. 'Ruby, are they here?'

The others all stared at me. Grandma grasped my arm, hard.

Ruby jutted out her chin, like she knew the answer but wouldn't tell.

'Ruby, did you bring them with you? When you found this place? Are my sister and my mother in this town?'

Ruby took off her hat and fanned herself briskly. 'It's hot out here. We'd better get you somewhere safe indoors. You can rest.'

'Ruby, tell us!' I shouted.

She nodded. 'I'll tell you everything you need to know.'

We got separated after that. I was so hungry and tired, though, I couldn't quite think straight about where we were going. Next thing I knew, I was sitting at a long table in a public refectory with Peter and Karl. Figures moved about us, putting metal plates down on the rough wood. There was a kind of spicy meat stew and prairie corn bread. The smells were delicious. They took me right back to being a kid and being at home. The smell of the blue-tinged corn bread alone made me tear up.

Peter was eating with gusto, and slurping the cider they set down in tankards before us. He was doing his best to fit in and not draw attention to himself, to his difference as a City dweller. But even so he seemed refined compared with the folk that moved around us, bringing us food and asking us questions.

All I wanted to know about was my family. Were they here? What was wrong with Ruby? If she was powerful here and if she had somehow made herself leader, then surely she would have looked after Ma and Hannah? An excitement was building up in me, making my shrunken stomach bubble like Christmas morning. But it was fear as well. I didn't like not knowing. It made me start to imagine terrible things…

After some time of quietly eating, bolting our food and not saying anything – even though I could see Peter was burning with questions – I realised that someone else was standing by our table. She wasn't respectful like the others, leaving us in peace. She was standing there, staring at us frankly.

I looked straight at her. There was no mistaking that pale, solemn face. That long, blonde hair. That prissy expression she always used to wear. Sure, she looked older, but it was still the same girl.

'Annabel!' I said, almost choking on the bread. 'You're here, as well!'

'Yes, we're here,' she said. Her voice was odd. Dull-sounding. A monotone. Her eyes were grey, staring into mine. 'The Adamses are back in charge of the Emporium. We're open for business again. These people were nothing more than peasants when we arrived here. Mother says we have brought them a little class and some distinction.'

'Your mother and father are here!' Now my heart was beating fast in my chest. I got up on my feet, and Annabel backed away, as if she thought I was about to grab her.

'My parents are in very good health,' she said. 'No thanks to you, Lora Robinson.'

I sighed. This again! 'Look, Annabel Adams, you saw how things were. I had no choice. I thought that I was buying your freedom by going to the City…'

The girl shrugged. She was back wearing all those ruffles like she used to wear. She looked dainty and prim. She looked like she'd fit right in with the likes of the Graveleys in the City Inside. Maybe they'd have been best off sending her there, instead of me.

'Annabel, my ma and my sister … you must tell me…'

'Are they here?' she quirked one eyebrow at me. 'Well, now. I'm not sure I'm allowed to divulge that information.' Then she turned smartly on her heel and marched from the room.

I was about to charge after her and box her ears, but Peter held me back. 'Probably not a good idea to get into brawls with our hosts.'

'Huh,' I said. The few bitefuls of food had revived me. Now I was spoiling for a fight. 'That ungrateful brat! She and her parents would all be dead now, probably, if I hadn't have led the way out of Our Town…'

The Martian Ghosts would have got them, wouldn't they? They'd have been Disappeared?

I sat down heavily on the bench. But was that even true? I'd assumed for so long that the story in my head was the right one: that those giggling ghosts meant us all harm, and they were seizing us, one by one, making away with us, and devouring every scrap of our mortal selves.

But now I kind of knew different, didn't I? I knew that some of the Disappeared wound up in the City Inside. They weren't eaten at all. They were just taken away to start a new life in the City.

So perhaps I hadn't saved anyone? Perhaps I had even made things worse for them?

'Lora, you look upset,' said Peter. 'You should calm down. I'm sure they'll tell you about your ma and sister before long...'

'I know,' I said. 'It's just ... I think I've done everything wrong, Peter. Maybe I should never have left home in the first place ... I'm starting to think every decision I've made along the way has been completely wrong...'

He shook his head. 'Not from where I'm sitting. If you'd stayed at home, and never come to the City Inside, then I'd never have met you, Lora Robinson. And you've been nothing but good for my life.'

'Thanks, Peter.'

'I mean it! I'd still be living in the Den, and busking ... and that's about it. That's all I was doing there.'

'Now, you're facing deadly danger every day and eating lizard broth…'

He blanched slightly. 'Lizard?'

24

We were there a few days in that town with no one telling us what was going on. It seemed that Grandma and Ruby were deep in talks, and they made it seem so grand and important. All I could picture was when I was a little girl and those two old ladies would talk up a storm together and it was never about anything important: it was just nattering on.

Dean Swiftnick went around the town in a kind of daze. I realised why. It was like this whole place was a living book. It was all there to be read by him and understood. It was knowledge for him to drink up. He wanted to be the wisest man on Mars and for his mind to contain it all.

Peter and me, we just lay low and got over the rigours of our journey to get there. The people weren't exactly madly friendly, but it was okay. They didn't seem to mean us any harm.

Then one day Peter met the prisoner and things changed.

He was out walking Karl, through the streets of the town. There wasn't very far to walk, but Karl liked to lollop around, getting his exercise and poking his cold, wet nose into every corner.

When they came back one day I could tell something had gone on. Peter looked – not shocked, exactly. Perturbed. He took me aside.

'I found someone … a man. A prisoner.'

I was on the alert straight away. 'I knew there was something shady going on here.' The townsfolk all looked shifty to me.

'We were passing by a row of empty houses. They looked like they'd been ruined in a storm or something, and abandoned, and Karl was sniffing and pawing at a certain door…'

Peter went on telling me the tale and I admit to feeling envious that I hadn't been there. I'd missed all this. 'What did you find?' I asked him, when he described setting foot inside the house. The desert sand had drifted into every room. From the furthest room he and Karl could hear a feeble voice.

'Hello..? Help me… They've left me here…' It was a strange accent. One Peter couldn't recognise.

'It was a man, Lora,' Peter said. His eyes were still wide with disbelief. 'And then again, it wasn't. It was a man with wings. An insect. He had huge, crumpled wings that lay crushed underneath him. They were mostly ruined tatters. He was laying on a small bed at the very back of the house. Everything was covered in thick red dust, including him and the ragged blanket that covered him. He was calling for help. He couldn't get up. I don't know how long he'd been calling out. He looked amazed when Karl and I walked in and saw him…'

I was sitting bolt upright, listening to this. 'Is he still there? You'd better take me, Peter. You'd better take me to him right away.'

His eyes were dark and smudgy, but I could see them watching me as we entered the room. The dust caught in my throat and made me gag. How could the prisoner even breathe in there, I wondered?

When I saw the cracked skin of his face and his chest and his skinny limbs I knew straight away he was kin with my friend. Even the patterns on his spoiled wings were similar to hers. The shades of gold, chocolate and indigo were dimmer, however, as if the soft velvet had worn away with the years.

His voice was low, it buzzed in our ears. You could tell he hadn't tried to talk in a long time.

'The boy said he – *koff koff* – would bring you.'

'I'll do what I can to help.'

'It's no good for me. It's too late now. *Koff koff*. But there are things I should tell you, things you need to know…'

Now I looked more closely I could see there was still light in those spiralling eyes. A flicker, not much more.

'Who did this to you?'

'They are terrified of me, that's why they hurt me,' he said.

'The townsfolk?' I asked. 'It was they who smashed you up?'

'I should have stayed away. It's all my own fault. I should have known – *koff koff* – that they would take fright. They saw the shadows I cast in the Earth light, even though I tried my hardest not to be seen. They stay awake and keep watch for what they call "ghosts". They are scared we will come and take them away and eat their flesh – *koff koff*.'

'The people of my town were the same,' I told him. 'We thought that's what was happening, too. We didn't know you were helping us, and carrying us off to the City Inside…'

The crumpled butterfly man had a coughing fit then, so violent that he was doubled up. His eyes went black and I thought we were going to watch him die. Peter and I took a step forward, as if to help, but there was nothing we could do.

Karl didn't like being in that room. He hung back by the door, scuffing in the drifted sand with his metal paws.

'I wasn't coming here to Disappear anyone,' the Martian man said. 'I wasn't going to eat anyone's flesh. I was coming to warn them. I thought I could talk to them. I knew that the old woman – Ruby – was intelligent and she might – *koff koff* – understand my warnings…'

'You knew Ruby, then?'

'I know of her.' Those dark, swirling eyes looked straight up at me. 'And of your whole family, Lora. *Koff koff.* I know about you all.'

'But … how?'

'I don't have time to explain it all. Suffice to say that my daughter – *koff koff* – has passed on everything she knows. We share the same mind, in many ways, and I know all about you, Lora. I know what you have faced.'

I stared in amazement at him. My skin was creeping and crawling as if at the touch of a thousand insect legs.

'Your daughter? Do you mean Sook? Are you telling me about Sook?'

Peter looked at me. 'You're making him agitated … he's coughing worse … Look, forget all the questions for now. We must get him out of here. Sir, can we help you up? Are your wings too spoiled to fly? Can you leave this town?'

It seemed hopeless to me. The old insect man was dying. Couldn't Peter see? And then it struck me that Peter never lost hope. In the time that I had known him, even last Christmas, he never lost hope. Even when he'd lost Karl and everything back in the City seemed so bleak, he had never given up.

'*Koff koff.*' The old man – Sook's father? – was struggling to say more. He told us, 'This is a bad place, you know. The ancient minds are calling out. They are reaching out … with tendrils of pure evil. They will take over the hearts of everyone within their grasp…'

'Ancient minds?' said Peter, in a hushed, awed voice. 'Who are they? Where are they?'

'Not far from here ... in the underworld vastness ... in the forests of the underworld and the palaces far below the crust of the desert. They have been sleeping there for such a long time. Now they are waking up, still dreaming and gloating and bloated with horrible plans. They are greedy and they are waking up so very hungrily ... *koff koff*...'

He was making no sense. He stared at us urgently, keen for us to heed his warning. But I think by then he had lost his mind.

'Tell me about Sook,' I said. 'Have you seen her? Has she come this way? Will I ever see her again?'

For a second it seemed he might have an answer. His twisted face softened into what I thought was a smile at the very mention of his daughter, my friend.

But then there came a crashing from the front of the derelict building. Karl yelped and I just about jumped out of my skin.

The men had found us. They came barging into that dusty house with weapons cocked. They sneered at us and seized us and looked down at the prisoner, who coughed and looked completely helpless.

The leader of the guards said: 'You shouldn't be here. No one is allowed to speak to this devil. Those are Ruby's orders. This infernal being is dangerous.'

'He's no such thing!' I burst out. 'He's injured. He might even be dying … You must tend to his wounds. You can't keep him prisoner, untended…'

The guards just laughed. They jeered at the Martian man.

'We dragged him out of the sky,' the leader smirked. 'We lassoed this creature out of the sky and pulled him down to the dirt. We wanted to pull off his wings and his arms and his legs. Have his kind ever shown our people any mercy? They preyed upon us. But old Ruby won't let us retaliate. She won't let us kill him because he is a puzzle. She says she wants to figure him out.'

The insect man was racked with coughs and they left him to it. They dragged Peter and me out of that house and back to where they could keep a close eye on us. Karl followed unhappily.

We were just as much prisoners as the butterfly man.

It was that night that they threw us into a cell with the others, in the town jail.

'What are they going to do with us?' Peter asked.

I really had no idea. Surely Ruby wouldn't let anyone here do us actual harm?

I realised that it was all down to Grandma now, and whether she could reach out to her old friend. Our lives were in the hands of two crazy old women.

In the cell Professor Swiftnick was waiting for us, looking downcast. Toaster and Barbra were both running on emergency reserves of power. No one had answered their pleas to let them recharge.

'All of this is fascinating from a historical and sociological point of view,' gabbled the professor. 'And, of course, I am delighted that we have found the object of our quest. But I could do with a warmer welcome, I must say.'

'Object of our quest?' asked Peter.

'He means Ruby,' I said, giving the old man a dirty look. 'That's all he was on the quest for. To find someone who knew more about the past than Grandma does. Someone whose memory isn't knackered yet. Well, I hope you're happy, Dean Swiftnick. It looks to me that Ruby's gone even crazier than Grandma. Her memories are probably of even less use…'

'I won't know until I talk to her,' he said, glumly.

'You think she's going to sit down and have a cosy chat with you? She'd sooner blow your head off!' I was being mean and I knew it. But I needed to shout at someone. I needed to make someone else upset.

I was shocked, then. Because the old professor started crying. Silently. Not sobbing or bawling out. But even in the dim light of that metal-walled cell it was plain to see – the fat tears running down his weather-beaten face.

'I think … we're going to die here … and never learn

the truth…' he said. 'I'll never learn anything again … No more secrets … Nothing…'

'There are no more secrets,' I said. 'That's it. We know them all now.'

But I was wrong.

I was so wrong about that.

25

We were left in the cell overnight. All we could hear within the thick walls was the noise of Toaster and Barbra, who had been allowed to recharge themselves. It was eerie, the way that Toaster muttered and spoke aloud in his sleep that night. I never knew Servos were supposed to do that. It was like something was jiggling free in his electronic brain. 'Margaret, Ruby, Thomas ... come away from there at once! Ruby ... your father is looking for you! You children must return to your quarters...'

The rest of our team tried to sleep on the sawdust floor, ignoring his ramblings.

I had no idea what was to become of us.

At last the dawn light came peeking through the gaps in the blacked-out windows. The air started lightening and, just as my eyes adjusted, there was a clanking of keys and then Grandma was shoved into the cell with us.

She looked about twice her age. She sat down heavily as Swiftnick made room for her on the single hard bunk.

Grandma said: 'I've talked with her all day and night. I've tried to get sense out of the old girl. But I'm sorry to say that Ruby has gone bananas.' She broke into tears.

We tried to ask questions and get more information out of her, but Grandma was passing out with tiredness.

I hugged her until she slept.

It was the first time I had hugged her since I was very small. It felt good, even in that awful place.

Grandma managed about half an hour of a deep doze before the men came for us.

'Uh, Lora,' said Peter, as we were led out of the jail and into the harshly bright daylight. 'They wouldn't do anything rash like killing us, would they? To put us out of the way?'

I was shocked. Even at our most frightened and desperate, the prairie dwellers and folk of Our Town would never have done anything so barbaric. But this lot … actually, I wasn't sure. I didn't know what they were capable of.

There were townsfolk out on the street, even this early. They were dressed in their finery. Sunday best. Was it Sunday? I didn't even know what day it was. That was how far we'd strayed from civilisation in our journey across the wilderness.

The women were in their smartest dresses and bonnets. They carried dainty parasols, hopeless against the brutal sun. And the men were in their cleanest and tidiest shirts and trousers. Some even wore jackets and ties.

When our captors pushed and shoved us down the middle of the street, the townsfolk stopped to stare at us.

All of this made me feel uncomfortable. Not quite scared yet. But I was on my way to feeling disturbed by their behaviour.

'Why, we're going to church,' said Swiftnick, pointing at the whitewashed building at the very edge of town. It was a grander building than we ever had in Our Town, with a taller, more graceful steeple. Sure enough, the men were guiding our way, none too gently, towards the church's open doors.

The queerest kind of music was coming from inside. Warbling. Tuneless, really. I'd never heard music like it before…

Maybe once. Maybe an echo of it, once. On the plains somewhere, a long time ago. At the edge of a dried-up lake of salt. Maybe I'd heard the thinnest whisper of music like this then?

'Ruby talked a lot about her religion last night,' Grandma said. 'I couldn't really make head nor tail of it…'

'Is she worshipping the Gods of Earth?' asked Swiftnick.

Grandma chuckled. 'I don't know what she thinks she's doing. But it seemed pretty odd to me. I think she's dabbling in things she ought best leave alone.'

We were shuffled into the church, where it seemed the whole of the town's population was gathering. None of them looked particularly cheerful about being there. They had their heads down as they took their places at the wooden pews. Our group was led right down to the front bench, where there was a display of flowers and fruit and vegetables and such. It was a pretty poor harvest. The flowers were all dry and stringy and the vegetables were hideous, wormy things. Jagged faces had been cut into the skins of the pumpkins and gourds.

And then we saw Ruby. She was dressed in her white suit again and she was in a kind of rapture. Eyes shut, kneeling in front of the audience. She was humming along with that music which, now that I looked around, I couldn't see where it was coming from. The music filled the dusty, sun-spangled air. It was rising out of the floorboards, and coming down through the vaulted roof.

The windows were colourful. I couldn't make out the shapes and patterns in them. They weren't like any religious pictures I had ever seen before. I stared and stared at the unlikely figures in the glass. And could that be right? I saw the fins and silver bodies of Spaceships. I saw the gold and crimson of gigantic flames. A ball of fire burned underneath the ground. Tiny figures were kneeling in front of it. I saw figures being fed into the flames. Figures with fear etched onto their faces. Spiralling eyes and butterfly wings. Scorched purple skin.

Then Ruby was on her feet and talking to the whole congregation.

'We have amongst us in Our Town today new people. New arrivals from beyond our furthest imaginings. People who have come a very great distance to be with us and enter our community.'

There was a stirring of interest and we could feel all the townsfolk craning to get a look at us. We felt so dirty and dishevelled in our horrible clothes. We hadn't been given the chance to clean ourselves up at all. Peter smiled at me nervously, clutching Karl to his chest. Both Grandma and Swiftnick looked suspicious and worried about what might happen next.

Toaster had started muttering under his breath again. 'Ruby, Ruby dear, and Margaret, come away from there … Oh, girls, do behave … What will your father say, Ruby?'

Ruby could surely hear him, but she paid no heed.

I saw Barbra reach out and clutch Toaster's clamp-like hand that was nearest her.

'Our visitors have seen other towns and other communities on this world,' said Ruby. 'And yes, I believe them when they say that they have even lived in a distant City. Somewhere so huge and magical that I don't suppose any of us simple folk could comprehend such a place. These are wise and sophisticated people who have come to stay with us.'

There was a bit more muttering and speculation in the air when she said this.

'But,' Ruby added. 'If these new folk want to share our lives here in Our Town, then they've got to learn our ways, don't they? They gotta learn to make their horizons less broad. They gotta learn less fancy ways. They need to know how it is we do things here…'

There was a change in her voice. A harsher edge. Something threatening in it. The congregation picked it up and some of them were starting to yell out in reply. 'Yeah! They surely do! Yes, ma'am!'

I looked around at the eager faces. I was startled to see some I recognised. Annabel Adams was there, in one of her lacy, fine dresses, just like in the old days. And of course she was sitting there with her parents. Her mother was starchy as ever, and careful not to catch my eye. She just shouted out, 'Yes, ma'am!' But Annabel's da, Vernon Adams, was looking straight back at me with gentle eyes. His moonlike face was set in an expression of sympathy.

I wanted to point them out to Grandma, but when I turned back I saw that she was on her feet.

'Ruby, what's all this foolishness about? You ain't religious, girl. You're the daughter of a Star Engineer! You believe in science … not fairy tales!'

There was a gasp of horror at the way she'd butted in. Men hurried over and forced Grandma to sit down. 'Don't touch her!' Swiftnick protested bravely. 'She's an old lady!'

Ruby tossed her head. 'I'll tell you what I don't believe in, Margaret Robinson. I don't believe in *us* anymore. Not the Earth people who came to Mars looking for a better life. We brought all our rubbish and our old ideas about scratching a living out of the dust with us. We ate the Martian creatures and we exhausted their soil and we changed the very air so that we could breathe it. And we lived like peasants and gave nothing back. No, I don't believe in us or old Earth anymore.'

'You're talking rubbish!' Grandma cried out, making everyone in the place gasp.

'I believe in the Ancient Ones,' Ruby cried out, holding up both arms, palms uppermost. Her congregation called out in response and started to cross themselves and do all kinds of genuflecting stuff. 'I believe in the original people of Mars.'

'What?' I found myself yelling over the murmuring noise. 'You mean the Martian Ghosts?'

Ruby screeched with laughter. 'Them? The Ghosts? They are nothing! They are just the echoes of a former civilisation. They are trash. They did about as much good as humans ever did. No, I am talking about a far older people. They go back much further and they live deep, deep inside a wilderness none of us can even fathom…'

'This is fascinating,' Professor Swiftnick muttered. 'The texts of the early British settlers spoke of the Ancient Folk. They said they were like gods … or somesuch … but we've always dismissed these ideas as myths or fantasies on the part of space-sickened travellers…'

'They are true gods,' Ruby was trembling and shouting at the top of her voice now. 'And that is whom we worship in Our Town. Only the Ancient Ones can keep us safe.'

'Safe! Safe! Safe!' The whole congregation took up the word as a chant. It rang around us, making it hard to even think.

'We must appease the Ancient Ones! We must tell them you are here!' Ruby shouted.

I didn't like the sound of this one bit.

But there came a distraction just then. Something that none of us were expecting.

Toaster was on his feet. He had struggled out of Barbra's restraining grasp and squeezed himself out of the pew and into the aisle. Now he was advancing on Ruby with both clamp-like hands extended.

She paused in her rapturous cries. 'What? What are you doing? What does this contraption think it's going to do?'

There was nothing we could do. Nothing could stop Toaster when he got an idea into his head. He was way too strong for any of us. He was only supposed to help us, but recently something had gone haywire in his brain. He hadn't been himself in such a long time.

Now he had Ruby pinioned in his arms and she was shrieking for the men to come and help her. The crowd around us was in uproar. We were frozen there, horrified and thrilled at the same time.

'Good boy, Toaster!' Grandma snarled. 'Give the old biddy a good shaking! Knock some sense into her crazy old head!'

'Oh dear, oh dear,' sobbed Barbra.

Smoke was starting to leak from behind Toaster's glass panels. There were nasty-looking sparks emanating from inside his joints. He was programmed never to hurt human beings, and there was great conflict going on within him now. I tried to get up on the stage to help.

'Toaster, no ... don't give them the excuse to hurt you...'

'Let me go!' howled Ruby.

Toaster warded off everyone in the place. Both metal hands had hold of Ruby's throat. 'Back off, everyone, if you would,' he said. 'I will kill her if you come any closer.'

There was a tense silence. An impasse.

Ruby whimpered. 'The Ancient Ones will strike you down.'

'There are no Ancient Ones,' said Toaster calmly. 'Or if such beings exist, I don't care. All I care about is my family. The people I have been charged with looking after. You – old woman – were once almost part of that family. The Robinsons were kind to you, even though you were shady and never told the whole truth.'

Could my ears be hearing this right? I stared at Toaster. Something had gone right with his circuitry at last! His old voice was back! He sounded just like the old Toaster again! He had come back to us, just in time!

'LET ME GO!' Ruby twisted in his grip.

'First you must tell us what we need to know,' said the sunbed. He wasn't about to be intimidated by anyone. 'Tell us where Lora's mother and sister are. That is what we came all this way to discover. We are on a quest to reunite the Robinson family. And you will tell us all you know. There will be no more pseudo mystical flim-flam and shenanigans. Tell us now. Where are the mother and the girl?'

A very crafty look came over Ruby's face. 'Why, I was on the point of telling you that, you foolish machine. If you'd only just listened, you would have learned everything you needed to know!'

'Tell us,' said Toaster.

'Sacrifices!' Ruby grinned. 'They were our sacrifices! When we first came to this town. And the Ancient Gods came to me from deep under the desert. And they came into my head and taught me all I know. And when the people here made me their Elder and their leader and gave up their wills to me. That's when the Ancient Ones asked for the sacrifice. They asked very specifically for the woman and the young girl. They wanted them for their very own.'

Grandma just about fell over in shock. I was holding her up.

'What? Ruby ... what did you do with them?'

'I had to do what the Ancient Ones wanted,' she said. 'I simply handed them over. We took them out to the swamplands of the north, the mother and the little girl, and we left them there. For the Ancient Ones to take. It was all that we could do.'

Toaster had relaxed his grip in shock.

Now the men who protected Ruby saw their chance and they darted forward. They wrenched their Elder out of the sunbed's grasp.

Then they all fell upon Toaster. He went down on top of the altar with an almighty crash. They picked up anything that came to hand and smashed and clubbed him in order to keep him down. There were flashes and crackles of light as he tried to fight back.

There was nothing we could do as more and more of the congregation surged forward to stamp on Toaster and smash him up. 'Blasphemer! Blasphemer!' they were all yelling.

Every member of our party was seized and dragged back out of the building.

On her stage at the front Ruby was laughing her head off. 'You'll never see them again!' she yelled at me. 'You'll never see your mother and your sister again!'

I turned back and glared at her for a long moment.

'Yes, I will,' I said in a low, determined voice. 'Just you wait.'

26

Dear Da,

I am giving this letter to Professor Swiftnick. I am hoping that Ruby will be true to her word and allow him to return to the City. She wants him off her hands, not liking the way he's got of poking his nose into everything. She doesn't want some book-writer knowing everything that goes on here.

I am trying to persuade Grandma to go with him, but so far she refuses. She's hoping to fix Toaster. She can't leave him lying here in the middle of nowhere, broken and all in bits. I can see her point. Even if she stays here on the prairie, Swiftnick will get this note to you, I hope.

I want to say everything is well. It kind of is. We're all still alive, at least.

But I'm setting off on a new journey. Peter is coming with me. Barbra offered to come along and protect us and help us. This was kind of her, but I think she'll be more use to Grandma and Toaster. Peter and I can look after ourselves.

We're setting off into a wilderness none of us know anything about. We're heading into these swamplands in the north Ruby was ranting and shouting about. Where the Ancient Folk live, deep in the forests under the ground.

It's where they took Ma and Hannah.

You'll understand, I know. If you were here instead of me, you'd be doing the same thing. You couldn't just leave them there. I know where they went and I've got to go and find them.

We're setting off today.

It's the next part of my quest.

Ruby is all in favour of our venturing out. At first this surprised me. I didn't trust how helpful she was being. She talked in a strange voice about us going out to the land of the Ancient Ones. I don't know. Maybe she's being helpful. Or maybe she's just sending us there as yet more sacrifices to appease those gods of hers.

But, whatever. We're going anyway.

We have to.

If there's something I need to do, then I do it. Whatever the danger. Whatever the odds. I can't stop now.

When they warn me I just shrug. I don't care about the dangers.

What's the alternative? Stay here in this town with these half-mad folk, scared in their homes and bullied by Ruby? Turn back to the City with the professor? The City where I never really fitted in anyway?

I know which direction I have to go in.

They've given us supplies to last us the journey to the

swamps. And they've given us two burden beasts. You'll be glad to know that I've named them Molly and George.

We're ready to go. We're setting off this morning. I'll sign off now, and give this to Swiftnick. He thinks we're mad. But Grandma doesn't. Grandma thinks we're doing exactly what's right. She says we must find the rest of our family. She says we have to be brave and clever and strong. That's what life is all about.

So here we go.

We're going today.

We're setting off into the next unknown.

Love,
Lora

Acknowledgements

Thanks to Penny Thomas and Janet Thomas and everyone at Firefly, and to Patricia Duncker.